SHADES OF BLACK

PA
Somerset County Library System
11767 Beechwood Street
Princess Anne, MD 21853
PRINCESS ANNE BRANCH

Carlos Anthony

James Lorimer and Company Ltd., Publishers
Toronto

Copyright © 2023 by Carlos Anthony

All rights reserved. No part of this book may be reproduced or transmitted in any form or by any means, electronic or mechanical, including photocopying, or by any information storage or retrieval system, without permission in writing from the publisher.

James Lorimer & Company Ltd., Publishers acknowledges funding support from the Ontario Arts Council (OAC), an agency of the Government of Ontario. We acknowledge the support of the Canada Council for the Arts, which last year invested $153 million to bring the arts to Canadians throughout the country. This project has been made possible in part by the Government of Canada and with the support of Ontario Creates.

Cover design: Tyler Cleroux
Cover illustration: Caroline Icardo

Library and Archives Canada Cataloguing in Publication

Title: Shades of black / Carlos Anthony.
Names: Anthony, Carlos, author.
Identifiers: Canadiana 20220485151 | ISBN 9781459417199 (softcover) | ISBN 9781459417267 (hardcover) | 9781459417397 (epub)
Subjects: LCGFT: Novels.
Classification: LCC PS8601.N65 S53 2023 | DDC jC813/.6—dc23

Published by:
James Lorimer & Company
Ltd., Publishers
117 Peter Street, Suite 304
Toronto, ON, Canada
M5V 0M3
www.lorimer.ca

Distributed in Canada by:
Formac Lorimer Books
5502 Atlantic Street
Halifax, NS, Canada
B3H 1G4
www.formaclorimerbooks.ca

Distributed in the US by:
Lerner Publisher Services
241 1st Ave. N.
Minneapolis, MN, USA
55401
www.lernerbooks.com

Printed and bound in Canada.

To all the young Black boys across the world who are challenged with being themselves because they desire to be accepted for who they are and fit in. I want you all to know that you are enough. This book is for you.

CHAPTER 1
DO YOU ONLY LIKE BLACK GIRLS

It's 8:45 in the morning at Rexdale Secondary School. The school's halls are full of uniformed students rushing to their classes. A fifteen-year-old skinny teen boy with braids stands alongside his locker holding a piece of paper in one hand as he spins the dial to the numbers on the paper "15-36-19." He pulls down on the lock, but it doesn't open. He looks at his watch for the time.

"Man, I'm going to be late on my first day in a new school!" he mumbles to himself.

He looks around, checking if anyone saw his failed attempt before returning to his lock. His eyes meet Desiree's. She's a tall, beautiful brown-skinned Jamaican girl who smiles at him. Desiree and her crew look like a squad of Black Barbies with their sewn-in weaves, the illusion of being born with straight hair. She stands out from the rest of her crew with hair that shines and distinct features that include a small button nose, full lips, a small waist, wide hips, and a raspy voice that comes with a whole lot of attitude. Though you can't tell by looking at her that she has any attitude, not with that innocent smile that makes you believe and agree with everything she says. A smile that makes you feel unnecessarily generous.

As soon as students walk by, blocking his view, Romero returns his gaze to his lock. He only glances every so often, trying not to make it so obvious that he's been checking her out. It's only a matter of time before their eyes meet. Romero can't help but smile. *She's perfect!* As he shyly looks away, Desiree's smile disappears, replaced by a frown and narrowed eyebrows as female students walk by and give her crew elevator eyes. They flinch as Desiree and her crew pretend to hit them, laughing the entire time. Eventually the girls walk away, intimidated and ashamed.

After another failed attempt, Romero looks back to see if Desiree can see him struggling. He smiles nervously as he jiggles the lock.

"Come on, come on!" he says to himself.

He continues to smile at her before a group of female students interrupt his view of her. The girls in the group lower their heads and cover them with their hands as they walk away. When Romero makes eye contact with Desiree again, he gives her a puzzled look. She looks at the group of girls ahead and shrugs. He shakes his head and continues to smile nervously as he pulls at his lock.

Desiree and her crew are the most popular girls in school, feared and envied by all girls because of the influence they have in sports, art, and academics. Teachers love them because their accolades make the school look good and provide an opportunity for additional funding. The school is a safety hazard that desperately needs renovations. Students take turns playing hopscotch in between the tiles and the holes in the uneven floors. The classroom ceilings are mouldy, the portables infested by rodents, the bathroom stalls and locker rooms tagged with graffiti. The showers are dirty and have low water pressure. The gymnasium floors are uneven and need to be replaced; it's the reason they never have any home games for basketball. The only time the gym is used is for presentations, volleyball games, and phys ed. The lack of funding makes the school the joke of Etobicoke.

Romero was one of three Black students at his old school. He remembers dating Lisa, the heavy-set white girl he was ashamed to be seen in public with. He quivers with disgust and refocuses his attention on the variety of beautiful women from different parts of South America, Africa, and the Caribbean that make him smile and feel anxious.

He feels like a kid in a candy store, and much like when he was a child, he can look but can't touch. He remembers being in a convenience store with his mother, reaching for a chocolate bar and getting slapped on his hand before he could grab it. She would wave her finger as a final warning, and he wouldn't test her.

Romero loves the look, smell, and sound of a girl, but he's always self-conscious of what to say. He's observed how Will Smith pursues girls on *The Fresh Prince of Bel Air* but never felt comfortable reenacting those pick-up lines. He feels girls would laugh in his face and tease him, call him the names his stepfather does. That his stepfather would be right about him in saying that he's a skinny, weak, wutless boy. So instead of facing rejection, Romero smiles but won't engage until they do, first.

Still, the validation he's received from their smiles is enough to make him feel attractive and accepted. This is his opportunity to have a fresh start in a new school. He doesn't have to be a nerd; he can be cool at this school and attract all types of girls. He continued to observe all the different shades, curves, and styles of girls that walked by.

Romero never had any trouble getting the attention of women; his problem was his shyness. The only reason he dated Lisa was because he was pressured into asking her out. He called Chase a friend, but the truth is Chase wasn't really nice to him. Chase would make fun of him when he brought curry to school. He would mimic an Indian accent and request that Romero share his curry. Romero felt alone watching everyone laugh. Being one of few people of colour, he never felt the courage to stand up for himself. So when Chase was doing something racist, ignorant, or stupid, Romero would just laugh and wait for the bell to ring or for some other distraction.

One day after gym at Romero's old school, the boys were changing out of their gym clothes.

"Lisa has big boobs!" Chase held his hands up to his chest as if he were holding basketballs. The laughter filled the locker room. Romero shook his head, laughing along.

"Bro, you know she likes you?"

"You should totally ask her out!"

All Romero could think about was the fat jokes his stepfather would make about Lisa if he saw them out holding hands or if Romero brought her home to introduce her to his family. He couldn't help but reflect on the fat jokes his stepfather had made about his mother and how they made him feel.

"Nah, man, she's not my type," Romero responded.

Chase got in Romero's face while the others circled him.

"Not your type?" he said, tilting his head.

Romero gulped, as the boys hovered around him.

"Do you only like Black girls?" Chase asked.

Chase's questioned triggered a flashback of when he was surrounded by his aunties in his mother's living room. They gave him a stern look and said, "If we ever see you out on the street with a white girl, we'll disown you."

Romero returned from his flashback and looked around the room to see his peers anticipating his answer.

Chase rolled up his gym clothes and put them in his pants. He started twerking. The boys in the locker room laughed. Romero shook his head as he laughed.

"What's the matter? Lisa don't got enough junk in the trunk?" Chase asked.

"Nah, I like all different kinds of girls, I'm just not attracted to her."

"But you haven't talked to any girls at the school, and the one girl that likes you, you don't like back? Something don't seem right."

Chase looked around the room. "Watch out, fellas, Romero might be playing for a different team."

The boys quickly covered themselves as Romero laughed off his embarrassment.

How bad could being Lisa's boyfriend be?

He started thinking back to his aunt's warning. Romero was concerned about her not meeting his family's cultural standards. He was afraid if his family saw him and Lisa holding hands in public, they would humiliate them.

He continued to imagine the consequences of his

actions. He visualized being teased and taunted at family gatherings, eventually leading to his exile, but the teasing he was experiencing daily from Chase finally made him reconsider. After weeks of being teased, he finally gave in and asked her out. She said yes, and hugged him.

The relationship didn't last long. Lisa got bored of not having anything in common with Romero and his lack of experience and dumped him. Although Romero wasn't deeply attracted to Lisa, he grew fond of being in a relationship. It felt special having someone care about him. He enjoyed the admiration he felt from his peers the moment they found out that he was going to experience sex for the first time and missed it. The attention Romero was getting on his first day from the girls at Rexdale reminded him of what felt like his glory days.

Before walking over to Desiree, he thinks about what he will say. He thinks about how he would want things to be different with her than with Lisa, and remembers watching Will Smith hit on several women on his sitcom.

He fantasizes about whispering in her ear and watching her giggle right before she grabs him, pushes him against a locker, and starts kissing him.

Once he returns back to reality, all he can think about is saying the wrong thing or tripping over his shoelaces while attempting to pursue her.

Coming to this school is the fresh start I need. I can be different here. I can be cool.

He continues to attempt to match up the numbers again. He pulls down on the lock, but it still doesn't open. She walks over to Romero, leans in, and whispers in his ear.

"It still won't open, huh?"

He's startled but plays it off.

"Sorry if I startled you."

He points to himself. "Me? You didn't startle me, it's this stupid lock."

"Maybe the third time's a charm."

It has been more than three attempts, but he doesn't want Desiree to know that.

He spins the dial on the lock. After another failed attempt, Desiree extends her hand; he gives her the paper from his hand, and steps aside. She turns the dial three times and then enters the numbers. She pulls … it opens.

Romero scratches the back of his head in disbelief. *She must think I'm a total loser*, he thinks.

"I guess I owe you one."

He places his bag on the floor and takes off his sweater. His shirt rises up, showing off his six-pack abs. Desiree smiles, looks at his tie, and tilts her head.

"Hmmm."

She lifts Romero's shirt collar and redoes his tie's knot. When she is finished, she pulls his collar down.

"Sorry, your tie was bothering me. You new here?"

"Is it that obvious?"

Desiree chuckles. "Yeah!"

Romero blushes, embarrassed.

"See you around," she says, before walking off with her crew.

A biracial, light-skinned fifteen-year-old walks up to Romero as he closes his locker. He tilts his head as he watches Desiree and her crew walk off.

"Damn, the things I'd do to be in detention with any of them."

Romero chuckles before picking up his backpack from the floor and putting it over his shoulder. They walk down the hall.

"I don't know if detention is necessary, since you can see all you need to do is not have your tie done to get their attention," Romero says, pointing to his tie.

Joel rolls his eyes. "Okay," he says with sarcasm. "My girl is feeling you, and she doesn't just feel anybody, but be careful. Not everything that glitters glows."

Romero makes a confused face. "What do you mean?"

"Let's just say her ex ended up in the hospital after thinking he could get away with two girlfriends."

Romero thinks about his long-distance relationship with his first Black girlfriend and summer crush, Simone. He pictures himself being caught holding her hand at the movie theatre line-up while Desiree approaches him with her crew.

Romero makes a worried face. "Well damn, but who would want to cheat on a girl who looks like her?"

His new friend shrugs, then raises his hand to shake hands with Romero. "I'm Joel, by the way, but you can call me JoJo."

CHAPTER 2
REGULAR BLACK

Romero extends his hand to give JoJo a firm handshake. Joel attempts to do a handshake, but Romero botches it.

Joel laughs. Romero smiles nervously. He's embarrassed and looks around to see if anyone is judging him.

"You're not from around here, are you?"

Romero nervously laughs to himself. *Is my Blackness going to be questioned because I don't know how to do this handshake?* Romero thinks as they continue down the hall.

A group of senior boys take turns dribbling a basketball in front of the principal's office. In between passing the ball to each other, John, Bryson, George, and Victor take turns catcalling the girls that walk by. A short, dark-skinned, beautiful Filipino girl with big, thick, gold hoop earrings, Katrina Baptista, walks down the hall wearing a kilt that barely covers her butt.

Katrina's bronze complexion looks as if it was dipped in honey; it shines off the reflection of the chipped paint on the lockers, giving her a glow. Her hair is drenched in mousse, giving it a wet, crimped look as if she just came out of the shower.

John catcalls Katrina. Romero and Joel stop to see how John's attempt works out. She turns her head and gives John a dirty look then continues. Victor, George, and Bryson laugh at John's failed attempt. They exacerbate his embarrassment by banging on lockers.

JoJo and Romero chuckle at the commotion. JoJo stops laughing once John's eyes land on him and Romero. John flounces over to Romero and drapes him up against the locker. JoJo steps aside.

"Do you think you could do better?" asks John.

"We weren't laughing at you. I told him a joke," JoJo says.

Romero gulps. He looks over at John's friends laughing at a distance. He sizes up John, noticing a difference in height of several inches.

This guy is going to kill me, but if I don't stand up for myself, then the whole school will think I'm a punk.

A tall, short-haired teacher in a pencil skirt and heels walks by, breaking the tension. John lowers Romero back to the ground and adjusts Romero's collar as the teacher passes. JoJo, Victor, George, and Bryson whistle as they look up at the ceiling, pretending to be on their best behaviour until she passes through the doors. Romero and John's eyes follow her until she exits. John grabs Romero's collar forcefully. When John looks back at Romero, he swings and hits John right in the face.

JoJo's jaw drops. Bryson's, George's, and Victor's eyes bulge in disbelief as John stammers.

"I know you're not going to let this sophomore lay hands on you," says George.

John clenches his fist then attacks Romero with body shots. Romero covers his face and brings his elbows up, blocking the shots. Romero creates distance and goes into a boxing stance. The bell rings and the principal comes out of the office. He looks over to John and Romero. John quickly stands alongside Romero with his arm over his shoulder and a large grin. He firmly grips Romero's traps.

"Showing up late to class on the first day is not a good way to start the school year guys," says principal Da Vinci firmly.

Romero exhales a huge sigh of relief and looks nervously toward John. John leans into Romero's ear. "We'll finish this later," he whispers intimidatingly.

Romero gulps and watches as John walks away with his group of friends. He makes eye contact with JoJo; they walk to class. When they arrive, most of the seats have been taken. Romero and Joel spot an open seat next to Katrina. They look at each other and then the seat. Romero beats JoJo to the seat.

He smiles at his accomplishment until he looks around and sees John with Bryson and George at the back of the class. John brings his hand across his neck, implying that Romero is dead. Romero thinks about the body shots that John swung. He imagines himself leaving the school in a stretcher.

Romero gulps and turns his attention to JoJo, who shrugs as he looks for another place to sit. Romero takes out his binder and pen. He places his backpack on his chair and then starts writing the date. His eyes drift from his paper and land on Katrina's smooth caramel-coloured legs. His pen slips through his fingertips, falling to the floor and landing near Katrina's shoes. She looks at him then down at the floor to see the pen. They both reach to pick up the pen and bump heads.

"Ouch."

"I'm sorry about that."

"It's okay!" she says, smiling. "I'm Katrina."

"I'm Romero." He looks around the room then at her paper to see the characters she's doodled in her notebook. "You got skills, what'd I miss?"

She smiles. "You didn't miss much."

A tall, heavyset white man writes his name on the chalkboard — *Mr. Logan* — and *Social Studies* beneath it. He draws a line down the centre and continues to write: *Girls give sex to receive love.* On the other side of the chalkboard: *Boys give love to receive sex.*

Katrina and Romero glance at the board and then at each other. She tucks her hair behind her ears and says, "I like your braids."

Romero catches himself grinning cheerfully. He licks his lips then looks at her up and down. "I like your hoop earrings and I think you're beautiful."

"Wait, you said your name was Romero?" Katrina says with raised eyebrows. "Are you Dominican?"

"Nah, my parents are from Guyana."

"Guyana? Oh, I thought you were regular Black," answers Katrina.

Romero has a confused look. "Regular Black?"

"You know, Trini or Jamaican."

Mr. Logan puts the chalk down and turns around, facing the class. He begins counting heads as he looks at a clipboard that has a list of students' names on it.

Katrina turns her attention to Mr. Logan; Romero looks in her direction, still processing what she said.

"Before we start today's lesson, I'm going to call out everyone's name. Please raise your hand once you hear your name." Mr. Logan goes through the list of names and checks off the names of the students that raise their hand. "Looks like we're still missing a few."

He puts down the clipboard and then points at the chalkboard. "Would you say this is true?"

He looks around the classroom for a volunteer and then looks in Romero's direction. "You, sir, with the fancy hairstyle."

Romero points to his chest. "Me?"

"Yes! You."

Mr. Logan points to the chalkboard. "Would you say this is true?" Romero reads the board before responding.

"Yes!"

"Why?"

"Because it's what we're trained to do. Look at all the rom-coms and sitcoms we watch. The males find unique ways of professing their love to girls."

"Except if you're a rapper or an athlete," interrupts Desmond, a dark-skinned fifteen-year-old seated at the back of the class, pulling out the braids from his hair. "First, you get the money, then you get the power, then you get the respect, and then bitches come flocking."

"Language!" responds Mr. Logan.

"My bad."

"And what happens if you don't get money, power, and respect?"

"Then you're lame."

Desmond and the students in the back of the class laugh and do handshakes.

"Is there a way of getting respect when you don't have money?" Mr. Logan asks.

"Hell nah, look at the way we treat our homeless.

Look at the way we treat our peers who don't follow the latest trends. We live in an age where if you don't have money, then you don't have anything."

Mr. Logan looks around the class for reactions to Desmond's statement. He lands at Katrina. "Do you agree with Desmond?"

The class fixes their attention on Katrina. Romero looks back at the class and glances at John then at the crucifix next to the clock. He opens up his binder and takes a pen out.

I know she said some ignorant shit about me being regular Black, but please don't let her agree with that boy at the back of the class. Please make her different from the other superficial girls.

Katrina twirls her hair while pondering. "I mean, he isn't lying. I don't want to mess with a guy who can't afford to take me to dinner. Plus, who *doesn't* want to be around someone who wears the latest designers?"

Why does it always have to be the pretty ones?

Romero nods in agreement and writes in his binder. Mr. Logan observes Romero taking notes.

"Is there something of value that Katrina said?"

Romero closes his binder and smiles nervously. *Why does this guy keep asking me questions? Like damn, it's my first day. There's like twenty-something kids in the class. Pick one of them.*

"Just want to document the different perspectives, sir."

Mr. Logan smiles. "Care to share with the class?"

"I think the class is capable of taking their own notes."

Mr. Logan makes a face that says *touché*, then walks over to the chalkboard and starts writing. Gordon Broach tiptoes into the classroom, holding a basketball under his arm. He looks around the class, doesn't see an open seat, and sits on the floor near Desmond. Mr. Logan turns around to see Desmond and Gordon do a handshake.

He clears his throat. "Care to explain yourself, sir?"

"Sorry, sir, I couldn't find my Q-tips!"

The class starts laughing.

"Do you think Principal Da Vinci could make an announcement to help me find my Q-tips? It's really hard to hear without cleaning out my ears," answers Gordon jokingly.

The class continues to laugh until Mr. Logan slams a book on Romero's desk.

"Gordon, you're strolling through class minutes before it's over—"

"—It's not my fault!" Gordon interrupts.

"Then whose fault is it? And can you please stand up? Why are you sitting on the floor?"

Gordon looks around the class. "Because there aren't any chairs to sit on, duh."

The class laughs.

"Besides," Gordon continues, "I'm looking out for

you. It would be inappropriate for me to sit on your lap."

The class erupts in laughter again. Desmond and some of the male students at the back of the class shake hands with Gordon.

"All right, settle down." Mr. Logan stops to count the heads. "I want everyone to get into groups of four and come up with reasons why you agree or disagree with the statements on the board."

The class hesitates at first.

"Don't be shy, come on, get into groups of four."

The sound of chairs being dragged around the floor fills the room as students form groups. Romero, Katrina, JoJo, and Gordon sit together in a group. Gordon looks up at the time.

"There's no point in doing this. By the time we get into anything the bell will ring."

"What else are we supposed to do to occupy our time before then?" asks Katrina.

Gordon looks around and sees that Mr. Logan is distracted talking to other students across the room. He gets up from his seat and quietly walks out of the room. JoJo, Romero, and Katrina watch him leave.

"Well, we heard Katrina's opinion. What do you think, JoJo?"

"I think love is for suckers."

Katrina makes an unimpressed face.

"But I would be able to change for a girl like you."

Katrina rolls her eyes. "As if I haven't heard that one before."

"Okay, everyone, I want to hear from you guys before the bell goes," says Mr. Logan.

He hand-picks different groups throughout the room, allowing each group to talk about their arguments.

The bell rings, interrupting Mr. Logan's chance of getting to Romero, Katrina, and JoJo.

"Where's Gordon?"

They shrug.

He throws his hands up in frustration and erases the board.

Romero looks behind and sees John staring at him, rubbing his hands together.

All I gotta do is take it one class at a time.

The students quickly pack up their bags and head for the exit. Romero cuts between a couple of students, leaving John behind.

CHAPTER 3
NO BLACK PEOPLE, HOW DID YOU SURVIVE?

Romero is walking a few paces ahead of John and his crew. He looks back at John.

Damn, I gotta pick up the pace.

He manoeuvres through various students cutting in between them as he walks down the hallway toward his next class. As he approaches a classroom, he looks between his timesheet and John, verifying he's in front of the right class before walking in. When he enters, he's greeted with a warm smile from the short-haired teacher from earlier.

Ms. Kowalski, Academic English is what she writes on the chalkboard. Romero salutes her. She smiles, and he finds a seat at the back of the class. He puts his binder up to hide his face.

I really hope he doesn't come in here.

John pops his head into the class, looking for Romero.

"Can I help you, John?" asks Ms. Kowalski.

"Nah, I'm good. I just wanted to catch a glance at the newbies," responds John.

Romero peeks over his binder. His eyes meet John's. Ms. Kowalski looks at Romero and then at John.

Please send him out of the class, please.

"If you don't hurry, you'll be late for your next class," says Ms. Kowalski.

"I just wanted to make sure that one of your students arrived safely," answers John.

"Oh, which one?" says Ms. Kowalski.

The binder falls flat on the desk, revealing Romero's face. John points to Romero at the back of the class. "That guy!"

Romero looks away, pretending to be engaged in a discussion with other students. Ms. Kowalski gives John an annoyed look. John nervously smiles.

Please send him on his way, please.

"He seems to be doing just fine," says Ms. Kowalski.

Ms. Kowalski looks at the clock above the door. She grabs the doorknob, closing the door after allowing a few more students to enter.

A couple of boys whistle as the girls walk in.

"Pull those kilts down, ladies," says Ms. Kowalski.

The girls roll their eyes, adjust their kilts, and sit. They take out their phones and check themselves out in their camera.

Ms. Kowalski shakes her head and walks to the centre of the room, counting heads. Romero looks up and sees John at the window, giving him the finger. Romero shakes his head. Ms. Kowalski glances over at John and sees. She gives him an angry look and walks toward the door. John runs off. She opens the door and sticks her head out. He's gone. She closes the door.

She points to the clock. "If you're not early, then you're late," she says, walking back to her desk.

She grabs a stick of chalk and begins writing on the board. Desmond enters the class with earbuds in, dancing. He accidentally slams the door but doesn't hear how loud it is because of how loud the music is turned up on his iPhone. The attention of the classroom shifts from the chalkboard to Desmond, who doesn't hear and continues to perform dancehall moves on the way to his desk. Ms. Kowalski gets up from her seat and walks over to Desmond. She taps him on the shoulder. He turns around and takes his earbuds out of his ears.

"You're late, and your music is too loud!" says Ms. Kowalski.

Desmond lowers the volume on his player, wraps the earbuds around it, and puts it back into his pocket. He looks at the clock, then back at Ms. Kowalski. He shrugs. Ms. Kowalski makes a face, suggesting that she's offended.

"My bad." He turns around, walks to the back of the class, and sits next to Romero.

Ms. Kowalski exhales deeply, then walks back to her desk and picks up a clipboard with a list of names attached. She hands it to one of the students at the front of the class.

"Check your name off and then pass the clipboard to the next student to do the same." She clears her throat. "Okay, class, there's a clipboard going around the class that has a list of names on it. Please only check off your name from the board so I know who is here. Once everyone has signed their name, I'd like to ask the last person with the clipboard to return it to me."

Students take the clipboard, check their name off, and pass it on. Ms. Kowalski starts writing on the board.

"Today we're going to do a short exercise. I want everyone to write me a 500-word short story on their summer experience."

"All this work on the first day? Damn, I thought we would get into groups and do some team building exercises," says Desmond.

"Team building exercises? That's not a bad idea," says Ms. Kowalski. "I'll tell you what, how about everyone get into groups and write a combined short story about your summer vacation experiences."

The class sighs.

"Thanks a lot," says a student with attitude.

"Okay, to be fair I'll give you until the end of the week to submit it."

Ms. Kowalski begins counting heads.

"Five hundred words among four people isn't hard, but keeping the structure of the story will be. Plus, it'll give me an opportunity to see where everyone's writing is at for this exercise."

The students look at each other, hesitating to get into groups. Ms. Kowalski claps her hands.

"Come on now, chop chop."

The students begin to move around in the classroom and form groups.

As Romero lowers his binder, he sees Desmond, who greets him with a nod. Desmond extends his hand to Romero. "Wha gwan?" he says in a Jamaican accent before they do a handshake. Romero messes up toward the end.

Damn, I messed up again.

Desmond laughs. "Oh, you don't know that one," he exclaims. "It's like this." Desmond shows him the handshake with his other hand, and Romero observes.

Damn, he makes it look easy.

"Let's try it again," Desmond says.

Here goes!

He extends his hand out. They attempt the handshake again.

"There you go, you got it!" Desmond begins drumming beats on his desk with his hand.

"I'm Desmond, by the way, but my boys call me Des."

Damn, I need a cool nickname. Hmm, how about Ro?

Nah, that's stupid.

"What up, Desmond! My friends call me Rome. How you liking the first day so far?"

Desmond looks around at the girls in the classroom. "Man, some of these girls have really filled out those bras and them Lululemon tights over the summer … But yeah, it's cool. This year has more potential than last year did. How you liking it?"

Romero thinks back to the first time he saw Desiree and then his altercation with John. "I'm definitely not mad at the potential this school has. My last school had, like, no Black people."

"No Black people? How'd you survive?" asks Desmond.

"Just hung out with the other people of colour and played sports. It's how I earned the respect of the white kids," responds Romero.

"Sports? What, you play hockey?" Desmond laughs.

Romero laughs along but thinks about his time playing for Michael Powers's hockey team.

"Nah, man, I wasn't trying to conform. I played for the basketball team," says Romero, chuckling.

"Oh, you can hoop?" asks Desmond, surprised.

I don't want to oversell my abilities and embarrass myself.

"A little bit," says Romero confidently.

"Can you dunk?"

"Not yet, but I can grab the rim," says a proud Romero.

"Okay, my boy got some hops. Thought them white

boys would have taken your game away and made you soft," Desmond continues.

"Not even, but being here feels like home."

"Yeah, how have our people been treating you since you've returned to the promised land?"

"Aside from the scuffle I got in earlier, it's been aight."

"Scuffle? Who trying to catch hands on the first day?"

"I think his name is John," replies Romero.

"That tall African in first period?" asks Desmond.

"Yeah, that's him."

"Why is he messing with you?"

"He's mad the shorties have been giving me more love than him," responds Romero.

"I can't stand a hater," Desmond says, flicking his wrist backwards as if throwing something away. "Don't worry about that bootleg Joel Embiid, I got your back. You going to ball tryouts after school?"

"They have ball tryouts on the first day?" asks a surprised Romero.

I wonder who else is going to be there. I hope I don't embarrass myself, because then I won't fit in and won't be popular.

Desmond laughs. "You didn't hear? Ever since Broach dropped fifty points on the defending champions in his first year and got scouted, Rexdale High is trying to be known as a *basketball school*! So now they want to get a head start developing the team. The joke is the school wants to invest in the ball team but doesn't even have a gym to play in!" He chuckles.

Romero thinks back to how he had excelled in basketball at his old school, but wonders if it will be different at a Black school, if his talent will measure up.

"Word?"

"Word!" confirms Desmond.

"So where would we practise or have tryouts?"

Desmond laughs. "We still hold tryouts and practise in our gym, but our home games are at Marion."

"Marion? Didn't that school get closed? And aren't all of their students at Carr now?" asks Romero.

"Most of them. Some of them went to NACI, West Humber, and we got a couple that came over here," Desmond says judgmentally.

"So we're playing in an abandoned school?"

"Yup!"

"That's ghetto," responds Romero with a puzzled look.

Desmond shrugs. "You think that's ghetto? Before Marion closed down, there was a shooting in the cafeteria."

"A shooting? In the cafeteria? Word, did anyone die?"

"Nah, lil' homie didn't die, but let's just say homie won't be walking anytime soon."

Romero has a shocked look. "Damn! You think that could happen here?"

Desmond shrugs. "Dunno man, anything's possible. This is Rexdale. Our hallways are full of kids wearing blue and red bandanas. The kids wearing the blue bandanas are from Rexdale, and the kids with the red bandanas are from the Jane strip. The tension is pretty thick, but with Jamestown being a stone's throw away, I don't think the Jane strip kids want any smoke."

Romero thinks back to his altercation with John and tries to remember if John wore a red or blue bandana.

"You think Broach will go pro?"

"My cousin Thomas says ever since Broach's performance last year, the school has been looking at athletes as a way to receive funding. Apparently, Principal Da Vinci got a new Benz last year," says Desmond.

"You think he got that because of Broach?"

"Dunno, but for a man who just went through a divorce and basically lost everything, the math is not mathing."

"How do you know all of his business?"

"His wife was talking shit about him at the nail salon when my aunty happened to be getting her nails done. My aunty ain't got nothing better to do than gossip," says Desmond, shaking his head in disappointment. "So Rexdale High has been trying to step up their game by getting a head start on the tryouts and practice."

"Damn, that's big! So why hasn't Broach moved to the states?" asks Romero, looking attentively at Desmond.

"He's too young, and there isn't anyone to take care of his mom ever since his dad got locked up."

"Damn, you just be knowing everybody's business. You and your aunt got more exclusives than CP24."

Desmond laughs and waves his finger. "Nah man, my cousin Thomas follows basketballbuzz.ca, and we played ball with Broach over the summer. He gave us the scoop on some heart-to-heart shit."

"Man, I wish I had known y'all would have tryouts today. I didn't bring any ball shorts or sneakers," says Romero.

"It's all good, Rome, I got an extra pair you can borrow."

"Aight, bet," says Romero.

Romero looks over at Desmond's paper. "Bro, you haven't written anything on your paper."

Desmond shrugs. "We have until the end of the week, right?"

The bell rings, and students get up from their desks and exit the class. Romero taps Desmond on the chest.

"Yo, I got to go to my locker and grab lunch. I'll see you in the cafe?"

But before Romero can reach his locker, John finds him, pushes him up against a locker. Desmond rushes over to Romero's defence, trying to hold back John's punch.

CHAPTER 4
FIGHT! FIGHT! FIGHT!

"Thought you could avoid me forever?" asks John, pinning Romero.

Fuck, do I wait for Desmond to jump in and help me, or do I swing and hope for the best?

Romero struggles to free himself from John's grip. A small crowd begins to form around the fight. Desmond tries to pull down John's hand.

"Yo, let him go!"

John grabs Desmond and pins him against the locker.

"It's two against one, we got this."

Bryson, Victor, and George stand a few feet away, laughing and pointing.

"Look at these nerds, getting beat up on the first day," says Bryson.

A stocky six-foot-four sixteen-year-old with braids walks down the staircase, throwing a basketball back and forth with Gordon Broach. Broach points at John, who is holding Desmond and Romero.

"Yo, Thomas, isn't that your cousin?" asks Broach.

Thomas shifts his focus onto John by the lockers.

He quickly opens the doors and rushes over to John, pushing through the crowd. He grabs John and throws him against the locker. Romero looks at Thomas with awe while adjusting his collar. Desmond confidently gets behind Thomas. Broach dribbles around Bryson and George. He performs a crossover on Victor, causing him to fall to the floor. Students in the crowd giggle as Victor gets up. Broach performs various dribbling tricks, causing Bryson and George to bump into each other. The crowd *ooh*s and *ahh*s as they try to take the ball away from Broach, but he dribbles circles around them, embarrassing them.

Damn, if all the boys at this school play half as good as him, I won't make the team. I'd hate to be those guys right now.

Thomas grabs John by the collar and lifts him against the locker. "What do you have against my cousin?"

John looks behind Thomas. He looks back and forth between Desmond and Romero.

"Which one of these guys is your cousin?" asks John nervously.

If Thomas says Desmond, does this mean that he'll let John go, and I'll have to fight him?

Thomas looks back at a nervous Romero, and Desmond, who has a smirk on his face.

"Both of them," says Thomas.

Desmond puts his arm around Romero. Romero smiles, feeling protected and accepted.

"See, told you I'd have your back," says Desmond.

John gives him a dirty look. Thomas pushes John against the locker.

"If you got a problem with my cousins, then you got a problem with me," says Thomas, pushing John's head against the locker.

"All right, all right," says John.

Thomas releases his collar and steps back.

John fixes his collar and walks toward Bryson, George, and Victor. Thomas and Gordon stare at John and his crew as they walk off to the cafeteria. Thomas, Desmond, and Broach laugh in unison.

"Did you see the look on John's face when you draped him up?" asks Desmond.

"Priceless," says Romero.

Romero extends his hand to initiate a handshake with Thomas.

"Hey Thomas, thanks for having my back there. I really appreciate it."

Thomas and Romero do the complicated handshake that Desmond taught him. He completes the handshake and smiles, feeling good about himself. "No worries, man, I hate bullies, and I'd be damned if I let anyone mess with my lil' cousin and his friends."

Romero taps Gordon on the chest. "You really are the truth. I've never seen anyone dribble around a group of guys like that. Yo, can you dunk?"

"Nah, but I'm getting pretty close, though. My wrist can go over the rim. I'm just a few inches away from dunking with the ball," says Broach.

As the boys walk to the cafeteria, there are stares and whispers from various students through the hallways. In front of the cafeteria are two sixteen-year-old boys, Jamarcus and Latrell, led by a fifteen-year-old light-skinned girl, Kalinda. She's dressed in baggy clothes and counting money. Their uniforms are two sizes bigger than they should be. They pair their oversize clothes with durags on their heads and blue bandanas sticking out of their pockets.

Just ahead of Romero, Broach, Desmond, and Thomas are two short, skinny Italian students with comb-over haircuts and Gucci belts. They look down, avoiding eye contact as they approach Latrell and Jamarcus. Latrell and Jamarcus hold out their hands, blocking them from entering.

Kalinda steps in front of Latrell and Jamarcus.

"Yo, let me and my friends here hold some change until next week?" asks Kalinda with a smile, pointing at Jamarcus and Latrell.

The two boys look up to Latrell and Jamarcus nervously before answering.

"Sorry I don't have any change," answers one.

"Then buy us some fries," demands Kalinda. She looks down to their belts and rubs their buckles. "I know you Gucci-wearing kids have money."

"Yeah, no problem," responds the boy, who nervously pulls away.

Kalinda jumps in front of the other one, pretending to hit him; he flinches.

Kalinda, Latrell, and Jamarcus laugh.

Kalinda raises her hand and twirls her finger. Latrell and Jamarcus step aside, allowing the two to pass. Kalinda, Latrell and Jamarcus watch them order their food.

"And don't be stingy with the ketchup," yells Kalinda.

One gives her a thumbs-up.

Thomas, Gordon, Desmond, and Romero arrive at the cafeteria.

"Buy me some food, T?" asks Kalinda, holding out her hand.

Thomas gives her a look, kisses his teeth, and starts laughing. "I should be asking you the same thing. You think I don't see you hustling these white kids?"

They share a laugh.

"Wha gwan?" asks Thomas.

"You know, just trying to eat and feed my crew," says Kalinda, pointing to Jamarcus and Latrell.

She gives them a nod, and they step aside allowing Thomas, Gordon, and Desmond to pass. Then Kalinda extends her hand, blocking Romero from entering.

"Who's the pretty boy?"

Romero gulps. Thomas turns around.

"Yo, he's good, that's my cousin still," says Thomas.

"Oh, I don't see much of a resemblance," says Kalinda.

Latrell and Jamarcus block the cafeteria entrance. Thomas kisses his teeth.

"There doesn't need to be a resemblance for us to be family," Thomas replies.

She ponders for a moment as Romero chuckles nervously and clenches his fists. A moment of tension and then…

Kalinda laughs and taps the chests of Latrell and Jamarcus. They start laughing. Romero releases his fists.

"You should have seen the look on your face, pretty boy," says Kalinda, holding Romero's shoulder.

He continues to laugh nervously. She twirls her finger. Latrell and Jamarcus step aside.

"You're all good, man," she says, stepping aside to allow Romero to pass.

As he passes, she slaps his ass. Romero turns around in surprise. She gives him a wink, then smirks. He looks at Latrell and Jamarcus, confused. They shrug and face the door, awaiting their next hustle.

Desmond, Broach, and Thomas laugh at Romero, who is approaching them to find a table.

"Looks like Kalinda *likes you*," says Thomas, puckering his lips like he's about to kiss Romero.

Romero pushes him away. "Ugh, aside from her being scary as hell, she's cute."

"You better not let her hear you say that. She might make you her bitch," says Desmond.

Everyone shares a laugh except Romero, who visualizes himself carrying Kalinda's books to class and buying her lunch.

"Why does she have so much influence?" Romero asks.

"Kalinda is a hood girl who's good at acting tough and intimidating people," says Thomas.

"How does she control those guys?"

"Those guys have known each other since elementary school. Kalinda's older brother supplies their older brothers with work. They're just using her to get closer to her brother," says Thomas.

"Work?"

Desmond, Gordon, and Thomas share a laugh.

"Them Catholic school have y'all sheltered," says Thomas. "Look around, people are on drugs right now."

Romero looks around the cafeteria. He sees a white girl putting Visine in her eyes. He sees a couple of kids sitting in the cafeteria with dark sunglasses on.

"I'm not paying you shit," says Mateo, a Latino student trying to get into the cafeteria.

Jamarcus and Latrell push him away from the door; he pushes back Jamarcus and throws a punch at Latrell.

A crowd forms around the cafeteria entrance, chanting. "FIGHT! FIGHT! FIGHT!"

Desmond stands up on the table and sees fists flying between Latrell and Mateo. A bunch of other Latino students jump in to balance the fight. There is a full-out brawl between Latinos and Black students at the front of the cafeteria. Thomas and Gordon stand; Romero looks over at Thomas.

"Are we supposed to jump in?"

"Nah, you and my cousin wait here. I'll check it out and try to defuse the situation," says Thomas.

As Thomas and Gordon walk toward the conflict, pushing past chanting students, a gun goes off. A bunch of female students scream. The crowd runs into the cafeteria, looking for shelter.

CHAPTER 5
THEY SHOT HIM!

Romero and Desmond hide under a table. They can see Mateo lying on the floor in a pool of blood coming from his leg, wincing in agony.

They shot him! I can't believe they shot him for lunch money!

Broach kneels alongside Mateo. He takes off his uniform sweater and tears off the sleeves. He wraps Mateo's leg with his sweater and ties the sleeves together. Mr. Logan arrives with two students. He kneels too.

"Are you okay?" asks Mr. Logan, looking at Mateo, who winces and nods.

"Everything is going to be okay, help is on the way," says Mr. Logan. "Do you know who did this, Gordon?"

"They went that way," says a student, pointing at the exit.

Mr. Logan gets up and runs to the exit. He stops once he hits the doors, out of breath. He passively pushes the doors open, searching for the suspects. After not being able to identify them, he comes back to Mateo.

"Gordon, did you see anything?" asks Mr. Logan.

"Why would I have seen anything? I wasn't here when he got shot," says Gordon.

"I don't know, son, you're at the scene of the crime, covered in blood. If the police were here, they would consider you a suspect," says Mr. Logan.

"Suspect?" asks Broach. He moves back. "Why would I be a suspect? He was like this when I got here."

"Relax, son, I'm not accusing you of doing anything," says Mr. Logan.

Broach narrows his eyes at the teacher. "Do I need a lawyer?"

"I don't know, son, let's wait until the police get here."

Broach gets up. "Nope, I'm not staying and waiting for the police to come, I know what y'all trying to do. You want to pin this on the first Black kid that you see. I could have just left him there and not tried to help him."

Gordon walks away at a fast pace. Sirens wail in the parking lot. A few students rush into the cafeteria, out of breath.

"The police are here," says one student.

"Yo, they're going to try to pin this on Broach and

mess up his chances of hooping in the league," says Desmond.

"Nah, we're going to clear him with the truth," says Romero.

"You talking about snitching?" asks Desmond. "We don't know who shot that kid. All we know is that the gunshot went off before Broach even got to the scene of the crime."

"Yo, where's your cousin?" asks Romero.

Desmond shrugs. "I don't know. I lost sight of him in the crowd."

Romero plays with his little chin hairs. Thomas probably ran after Kalinda to investigate what went wrong and how to help her out of this situation, he thinks.

"Maybe he ran after Kalinda and her crew."

Desmond extends his hand to Romero and pulls him up on his feet. "Let's go find them," he says. "This ain't got nothing to do with you, so if you want to walk away, I understand."

Romero thinks back to when Thomas claimed him as his cousin, and when Desmond promised to have his back.

"Nah, forget that. Y'all had my back with John, so I'm ride or die."

The boys do their handshake and walk out of the cafeteria. Mr. Da Vinci arrives at the cafeteria with six police officers carrying assault rifles over their shoulders.

Romero's and Desmond's eyes widen.

Why do they need assault rifles in a high school, and why so many police officers for just three kids?

Mr. Da Vinci walks into the cafeteria, looking at Desmond and Romero suspiciously.

"Classes have been cancelled for the rest of the day. Everyone in the cafeteria at the time of assault will be expected to cooperate with these officers, fully," says Mr. Da Vinci.

"I don't have to do or say shit. I know my rights. I wanna talk to my parents, and I wanna lawyer," demands Desmond.

He looks over to Romero and sees sweat dripping from his forehead.

Romero thinks back to the TV show *Cops* and how the police would tackle the suspect if they tried to run. He thinks back to the stories of Rodney King and the stories that his cousins told him about officers planting drugs on them to send them to prison.

But none of that scares Romero more than going to jail. Mr. Da Vinci can see the sweat dripping down his face and raises an eyebrow. "Are you okay?" he asks suspiciously.

"I'm not feeling well," says Romero.

"The sooner everyone cooperates, the sooner everyone gets to go home," says Mr. Da Vinci.

Paramedics arrive with a stretcher to take Mateo out of the school. Mr. Logan follows the paramedics outside.

Meanwhile the police officers enter the cafeteria and grab seats, place pens and papers on the table before them.

"All right, everyone, form a line. I don't got all day," says one police officer.

The students get into lines, waiting to be questioned.

"Did the victim have any enemies?"

"Once I heard the gunshots, I just ran for cover."

"Do you know what the victim was doing at the time of the assault?"

"All I heard was arguing, then I saw pushing, the next thing I know there were gunshots and people started running."

Romero and Desmond are next in line to speak to the officers. The officer beckons Romero over with his finger. He looks over to Desmond, then slowly walks to the police officer. He takes a seat.

All I got to do is answer his questions and it will all be over. I won't need to snitch because I didn't actually see what happened.

"Were you present during the shooting?" asked the officer.

"I was in the cafeteria eating when it happened," answers Romero.

"Did you see who was involved in the shooting?"

"No, I heard shots. The next thing I know, people are running for cover, hiding under desks."

"Okay, you're free to go, but I'll need you to leave your name and number in case we have any follow-up questions."

Romero nods, acknowledging he understands. He walks away, looking at Desmond on his way out. Broach is being escorted by force into the cafeteria by officers; Principal Da Vinci trails behind.

"Look, Gordon, you can either cooperate with these officers here or you can take a ride down to the police station," says Mr. Da Vinci.

"I'd like to call my mom and have her present while I'm being questioned," says Gordon.

"Sounds guilty to me," says one officer.

"Let's throw him in the cruiser until his mother arrives, maybe he'll change his mind," says another officer.

Broach looks worried as the officers escort him out of the school and into the back of a police car.

CHAPTER 6
I CAN'T GO TO JAIL

Thomas is running after Kalinda, Jamarcus, and Latrell He chases them into a McDonald's. Once inside, he uses the door to stabilize himself. He puts his hands on his knees and continues panting.

"What the hell happened back there?" asks Thomas.

"Look, Thomas, it was an accident. We didn't know that he was going to fight back," Kalinda says.

Thomas looks at her, surprised. "Fight back? How could you think that everyone in the school was going to put up with your shit? Not everyone is going to be afraid of you guys."

Kalinda paces back and forth with her hands on her head. "What was I supposed to do? I can't have people thinking they can get away without paying me."

"So you shot him?"

Kalinda looks around the room to see if anyone heard Thomas. She sees a few students at a table looking in her direction.

"Lower your voice, Thomas. I didn't shoot anyone," Kalinda aggressively whispers. Then she turns to the students and yells: "WHAT ARE YOU LOOKING AT!" The students look away at once. The manager observes the commotion from the cash register.

"You're the one that's out here yelling at people, drawing attention to yourself — the fuck," says Thomas, shaking his head. "What are you going to do?"

"We're going to lay low for a bit," says Kalinda.

The restaurant manager walks over to Kalinda.

"If you're not going to order something, then I'd like to ask you and your friends here to leave."

Kalinda cuts her eyes at the manager.

"Look, either order or get out." She points to the door.

But Kalinda, Thomas, Jamarcus, and Latrell don't budge, only narrow their eyes at the manager.

"Look, if you guys don't get out, I'll call the cops."

"Call the cops for what?" asks Kalinda. "We haven't decided on what we wanted to order. For fuck's sake, we've only been here for a couple of minutes."

Kalinda gets out of the booth and starts pacing. Thomas reaches in his pocket and pulls out a toonie, tossing it in the manager's direction.

"Get me a vanilla cone," he requests with a smirk.

The manager slides the coin back to Thomas. "We're all out of ice cream. Besides, that's not how things work here. If you want to order, you have to place it at the front."

"What difference does it make if we pay here or there?" asks Thomas. "You went through all this trouble to visit us at our table telling us to order, and you're not going to take my order?"

"Sir, if you want to place an order, one of our cashiers will assist you at the front," says the manager.

Thomas looks up and puts his hand to his mouth, pondering. The manager looks at Thomas, waiting for him to get up.

"You know, I'm not sure if I still want that ice cream cone. I might want to get the two apple pies for a dollar twenty-nine," answers Thomas.

The manager exhales deeply. "The ice cream machine is down."

"How come y'all's ice cream machine is always down? What's the point of offering a product if it's never available? You know what, don't answer that. Look, I know you have a restaurant to run. Would you mind if I had a few more minutes to think about what I and my friends want to eat?"

"Is this happening because we are the only Black people here?" Kalinda chimes in.

The manager clenches her fist and walks away. Desmond and Romero walk into the McDonald's.

"Yo, school's cancelled for the rest of the day, and the boi dem are questioning students," explains Desmond.

"Fuck, the boi dem are there already?" asks Kalinda.

"Yeah, man, they're looking for whoever shot that Latino kid in the leg," answers Romero.

Kalinda gets up from her seat and into the faces of Romero and Desmond. "Did y'all snitch?"

"How could we? We didn't see anything," responds Romero. Kalinda looks at Desmond for confirmation.

"Most of the students pretty much said the same thing — they all heard a gun go off, then heard screaming and saw people running," says Desmond.

Kalinda sits down and looks up to the ceiling. "Fuck," she says.

"What are y'all going to do?" asks Romero.

"That's what we're trying to figure out right now," answers Kalinda with attitude.

"Why don't we figure out what the worst-case scenario would be? You guys are minors, right? How bad could things really be?" asks Romero.

Kalinda holds her hand to her face. "Hmm ... wasn't Smokey in juvie for stabbing up that guy last year?"

"Yeah, the kid was so scared. He didn't want to press charges, but the boi dem had camera footage," says Jamarcus.

"He only did a few months, but he said the things he saw in there were messed up. He said mans would be straight weeping at night," Latrell adds.

"You got to have friends when you're on the other side, otherwise mans will get offed or emasculated," says Jamarcus.

Maybe if I give them legal advice, they will respect me. Maybe they'll think I'm on their side, and they'll be nice to me. Maybe I can earn their respect. Let me feel out the room, ask a question and see where things go.

"Where's the Glock?" asks Romero.

Kalinda walks up to Romero. She stands in front of him, giving him elevator eyes.

"Don't ask questions you don't want to know the answer to. It's in a safe place," she says.

After canvassing the people in the room, Romero notices Jamarcus putting a backpack over his shoulder.

The gun's in the bag.

Kalinda smiles, then starts laughing; everyone looks at her as if she's lost her mind.

"Yo, how could you be laughing at a time like this?" asks Latrell.

"They ain't got no footage," says Kalinda. "If they have no proof, they can't charge us. All we got to do is lie and say we weren't there. The people that can ID us aren't going to snitch. If they do, we'll get them to change their story."

"What makes you think they'll listen?" asks Desmond.

"I don't think anyone is going to mess with us — they already think we intentionally shot that kid. And if they know what's good for them, they'll stay quiet."

Romero loosens his collar.

Kalinda walks up to him. "Right, pretty boy?"

Romero gulps. "Right."

I hope they don't think I would snitch.

Kalinda punches him on the arm. Romero rubs the spot.

Ouch! That hurt. Gotta play it off like it didn't, though.

"Good man," she says.

"So … what do we do now?" Jamarcus asks.

"We go back to school," answers Kalinda with a grin. "And when people ask us what happened, we say…"

"We say nothing — we don't know what happened, we weren't there. We tell everyone we were at McDonald's having lunch, and when Desmond and the pretty boy came here, that's when we heard what happened at school."

Jamarcus and Latrell smile. They move their hands up and down, snapping their fingers.

"Yo, that's why she's in charge. She's brilliant. All we got to do is lie and get everyone else to lie for us. Then we're good," says Latrell.

Sirens wail in the background. Two police officers enter the McDonald's. The manager walks over to the police officers. She points to the table where Kalinda and the boys are seated. Kalinda sees the manager point in her direction and looks back to the group.

"RUN!"

Everyone looks at the police officers talking to the manager and then bolts to the exit. The officers go after the boys. Latrell bumps into a chair and falls. Romero looks back, meeting Latrell's eyes. He watches as an officer puts handcuffs on him. The other officer continues to chase the group.

I don't want to go to jail…!

The police officer is gaining on Jamarcus as he struggles to hold his pants up and secure his backpack as he runs. He trips on a shoelace and falls down, dropping the backpack on the floor. The gun is revealed.

Kalinda looks back and sees Jamarcus on the floor, gun revealed. She looks at the police officer catching up and runs back for the bag. She tucks the gun back in the bag, zips it up, and puts it over her shoulder then sprints away from the officer. The officer just misses grabbing the bag, but catches Jamarcus instead.

CHAPTER 7
I NEED A FAVOUR

Kalinda, Romero, Desmond, and Thomas arrive at school to see multiple police cars parked at the entrances. They hide behind a car in the parking lot.

"Oh man, there's more now," says Romero.

They got Latrell and Jamarcus. Kalinda has the gun. We're all likely going to jail.

"Fuck," says Kalinda.

"You can't go back to school, Kalinda. There's too much heat. You got to go home," says Thomas.

Kalinda gets teary-eyed. "What if they're at my house waiting for me? Jamarcus and Latrell just got sucked on the way here. They were right behind us!"

Kalinda breaks down in tears.

She looks stressed. Maybe if I offer her a hug and be there for her, she'll be nice to me. She looks as scared as I feel.

Romero opens his arms; she embraces him, crying into his chest.

I didn't think girls like her could cry.

Thomas and Desmond smile, wink at Romero.

Why do these guys gotta be like that? They probably think I'm trying to smash. Then again, she could look different in a kilt...

She pulls away, catching him smiling back at Thomas and Desmond, then hits him on the arm.

Damn, I've been made. But I can't keep letting her hit me like this. If I ask her to stop, she might think I'm weak and keep doing it. Maybe I can turn this around, or maybe I should try to appeal to her vulnerable side by letting down my defences.

"Ouch! What was that for?"

"Listen, I'm not some girl that's going to fall for your charm," says Kalinda. "You don't think I don't see your game? You're doing the sensitive guy thing."

She pushes Romero's head back with her trigger fingers.

I feel like a loser for allowing her to disrespect me in front of Desmond and Thomas. This is worse then getting my ass kicked by John.

Desmond and Thomas cover their mouths with their fists. "Ooooooh."

Let's try letting down my defences again. I really don't want to fight, because if I hit her, then I'll lose even more respect.

Romero puts up his arms, surrendering. "I was just being nice. This is a lot to be happening on the first day. If I was in your situation, I'd be freaking out right now."

"Well, you're not. As a matter of fact, you can dip home," says Kalinda, pointing to the bus stop.

All I'm trying to do is help!

Romero looks at her, confused. Thomas and Desmond share looks with Kalinda and Romero. Romero waits for them to say something, but after a moment of awkward silence he walks away.

Are they going to tell me to stay? We're supposed to be as close as cousins. Surely Thomas can explain to her that my intentions are good. Wow, this is taking too long ... you know what, Imma head out.

"WAIT!" Kalinda exclaims.

I knew she'd come to her senses.

Kalinda leaves Desmond and Thomas and runs over to Romero.

"I'm sorry. This whole mess has me stressed."

"It's all good," says Romero, scratching the back of his neck.

Kalinda holds her arm and looks away. "So, listen ... I need a favour."

She extends the backpack to Romero, who looks at Kalinda, then at the backpack, nervously.

I hope she's not asking me to do what I think she's asking me to do...

"I need you to take this home with you and hide it until things blow over."

"Hell nah!" Romero says. "Are you crazy? My mother would kill me if I brought a gun home."

Kalinda bats her eyes and pouts at Romero while touching his arm.

She's just using me. She doesn't really care about me. I can put an end to this. But what if this is my opportunity to earn her respect...?

"Please, pretty boy, if you do me this favour, I'll owe you a favour," she says.

"I don't know," says Romero, looking to Thomas and Desmond for confirmation.

This could be a great way to earn their respect, but my parents would literally beat me up for bringing home a gun. They would think that I'm in a gang or that I've fallen under negative influence. They wouldn't understand the circumstances or be able to see me as someone trying to help.

"I really don't want any smoke with my parents. Things are bad enough as is," he says.

Kalinda turns her back to Romero and starts walking back to Thomas and Desmond.

"Fine, if you're a scared pussy, just say so."

Romero exhales deeply, watching Kalinda walk off.

I guess I'll just prepare to deal with John tomorrow on my own.

He hangs his head, turns around, and walks home.

* * *

Kalinda turns around and shakes her head when she sees that Romero is really gone.

"Look, we all know I'm hot right now. But I really need you guys to take this home. Y'all don't even live that far. You can walk back," she continues, holding up the bag to Thomas and Desmond.

They both hesitate; Thomas gets out his phone, pulls up the TTC app.

"There's a bus coming in the next ten minutes. If you can get across the street on time, it could be a clean break."

Thomas looks around to see if anyone can see him. He grabs the backpack and unzips it, puts his hand inside the backpack, and pulls out the gun. He checks the safety and then takes a test shot at the grass.

Everyone is relieved when the gun doesn't go off. Thomas raises his shirt, puts the gun in his pants and pulls down his shirt.

"I got you, but you owe me."

"Whatever you want, T," says Kalinda. She sees the bus coming. "I got to go!"

She hugs Desmond and then Thomas. She puts the backpack over her shoulder, then puts her hood up. She looks for officers before she comes out from behind the car, then bolts for the bus stop. She misses the bus but continues to run after it, waving, to get the drivers attention. The bus stops, she gets on, and it drives off.

* * *

Thomas and Desmond run as fast as they can. When they arrive at the apartment, they collapse in the lobby. Thomas puts his fob against the sensor, opening the entrance door. He and Desmond take a look back to see if they were followed before walking inside. They press the button for the elevator, which is currently at the top floor.

"Let's just take the stairs."

Desmond continues to catch his breath. "The stairs? Fuck, man, haven't we done enough exercise?"

"Would you have been this out of breath if we had tryouts today?"

Desmond sighs and kisses his teeth. "Fine, let's take the stupid stairs."

Thomas and Desmond start running up the stairs, and by the second floor they are out breath.

"Pleeeaase, Thomas, can we just wait for the elevator on this floor? I'm sure we're out of sight."

Thomas places his hand on Desmond's shoulder. "Just a couple more floors."

Thomas walks up the stairs, holding on to the rails. Desmond hesitates at first, then follows Thomas shortly after.

They finally reach their floor. Thomas pushes the keys through the door. His mother, Brenda, is sitting in a chair wearing a bathrobe, rocking back and forth, a belt in her hand.

Thomas and Desmond tremble with fear. She stands to her feet and hits the arm of the couch with the belt.

"What's wrong, Mommy?" asks Thomas nervously.

"You forgot to pick up Kiyan from school. Now, before I whoop your ass, I want you to tell me why you guys have come home so late. School finished hours ago," asks Brenda.

"There was a shooting at the school," says Thomas.

Brenda starts breaking down crying. "I was so scared that something happened to you. I told myself that I was going to whoop your ass if you were all right."

Thomas looks at the belt in his mother's hand. He hesitates to comfort her. Brenda dries her tears and then calls Thomas and Desmond over with her hands. She drops the belt in the chair; they look at each other and nod, then walk over. She continues to cry and smile. When Thomas and Desmond get close enough, she hugs them.

"A mother's biggest fear is having to bury her child. The child is supposed to bury the parent, not the other way around."

Thomas and Desmond hug her back, looking at each other. Brenda looks up at her son.

"Why did y'all come home so late? What were y'all doing?"

"We were at McDonald's having lunch, thank God," says Thomas.

"Yeah, some students arrived at the restaurant and told us about the shooting," says Desmond.

"Did anyone die?" asks Brenda.

"Nah, they got shot in the leg," Desmond answers.

Thomas pulls away.

"What's wrong?" Brenda asks.

"Need to use the bathroom, that McDonald's is making my belly run," says Thomas.

Brenda shakes her head. "I told y'all about eating junk food."

Thomas runs to the bathroom, locks the door behind him.

He looks in the mirror, then at the toilet. He raises the toilet bowl cover and places it on the seat. He lifts up his shirt, takes out the gun from his pants, and puts it in the toilet bowl, accidentally breaking the toilet bowl chain but not noticing. He covers the toilet bowl, washes his hands, and exits the bathroom.

Thomas walks into his room and shuts the door.

"THOMAS?"

"Yes, Mom?"

"You forgot to turn off the bathroom light and flush the toilet."

He sighs, exits the bedroom, turns off the bathroom light. He returns to his room and closes the door.

"I didn't flush the toilet because I didn't use it. It was just gas."

Desmond lays on a bed, throwing a basketball up in the air.

"You stashed the Glock?"

"Shhhhh, lower your voice, man. If I go down, please believe I'm taking you down with me."

"My bad," says Desmond.

"I put it in the toilet bowl," says Thomas.

"What if she checks the toilet bowl?" asks Desmond.

"Why would she check the toilet bowl?" asks Thomas, irritated.

Desmond stops throwing the ball up and sits up. He shrugs. They hear Thomas's mother go into the bathroom, flick on the light switch, and close the door.

After a few moments, Brenda yells, "Thomas, can you watch one of them YouTube videos? The toilet ain't flushing!"

CHAPTER 8
WHY DO I EVEN BOTHER TRYING?

Inside his suburban home, Romero is lying on the bottom bunk bed with a phone to his ear. His ten-year-old nosy brother Leonard sits up on the top bunk playing video games. He lifts one side of the headphones off his ear, eavesdropping on the conversation.

Honestly, after the day I had, I need to feel better, thought Romero. *I wish Simone didn't live all the way in Pickering. I miss the moments we shared over the summer. She's like the hottest girl I've ever made out with, and if I was going to lose my virginity to anyone, I would want it to be with her.*

"How was your first day of school?" he asks.

"It was a bit overwhelming," says Simone. "But I'm happy that I have some of my friends from my elementary school."

Romero gets up and looks outside his room to see if anyone can hear him. After seeing his mother distracted by the television, he closes his bedroom door. Leonard sits up and watches Romero exit the room. He places the headphones over his free ear and continues playing video games.

Romero mutes the phone. He is about to pour his heart out to this girl and really doesn't need anyone interrupting the mood he is trying to set.

"Hey, Leonard?"

Leonard doesn't answer, continues to play video games. Romero unmutes the phone.

"I miss you," he says.

"I miss you, too," says Simone.

Leonard sits up on the top bunk, blowing kisses and making faces at Romero. "Ooooh, you miss her? I'm going to tell Mom you have a girlfriend."

Romero rolls his eyes. "Shut up! Ugh, I wish I had more privacy."

She giggles. "Awww, your little brother is so cute."

"There's nothing cute about him. I wish I was an only child," says Romero.

"Don't say that, it's mean."

"Fine, I'm sorry, he's just so annoying," replies Romero, sighing.

Romero takes a closer look at Leonard's outfit. "Hey, isn't that my basketball jersey?"

Leonard puts a sheet over himself. Romero lifts the sheet and inspects the jersey. He spots a ketchup stain.

"You got ketchup on my jersey?"

He attempts to take the jersey off Leonard but tears it as Leonard runs out of the room.

That jersey is the only thing I have from my biological father's side of the family. This is so frustrating. I can't have anything nice to myself. My brothers get away with murder, and I'm the only one that gets disciplined. Hate this house. Hate this family. I wish I was adopted.

Romero exhales deeply before slamming the door hard. His mother rushes into the room.

"Who's slamming doors in my house?" she asks with her hand up, ready to hit him.

Romero looks at her with fear and thinks back to a memory of her slapping him in the face; then another memory of being beaten with a belt in the shower.

"I'm sorry. I was upset. Leonard tore my jersey that Uncle Stacks gave me."

"You don't pay bills in this house, so you shouldn't be slamming doors. Slam another door and see what happens."

What about the fact that Leonard tore my jersey? Does she even care? I wish my father never died. I wish I didn't feel misplaced within my own family. It's not my fault things are tough financially. I never asked to be here. Well, at least I have Simone.

"I said I was sorry, Mom. Can't you see I'm on the phone?" he says nervously, holding his hand to the phone, muffling the sound.

She kisses her teeth, rolls her eyes, and exits the room, slamming the door. Romero jumps at the sound.

She told me not to slam the door and then she goes ahead and slams it. What a hypocrite.

"See what I'm talking about? Not only did he get ketchup on my Allen Iverson jersey, but now there is a tear on the jersey because of him."

"It's just a jersey," says Simone.

"Maybe to you, but it was given to me by my uncle, who's the only connection I have to my bio father," says Romero.

"When was the last time you hung out with him?" asks Simone.

"It's been a minute. Last time I saw him he showed me a crack rock, so I know he's probably busy trapping."

"Anyway, I've been thinking about our long-distance relationship and feel since we're in our first year of high school, we should explore," says Simone.

Romero paces the room; he doesn't respond.

Today is the worst day of my life. The altercation with John, a full day of disrespect at school, my jersey, my mom, and now this. Why now? I can't take this heartbreak right now. I need her.

"Hello?" says Simone.

"I don't get it. We had an amazing summer. I thought you loved me. Why would you want to explore if you love me?" asks Romero.

Simone sighs. "I don't get to see you. It was hard enough seeing each other over the summer, and I'm tired of waiting to kiss or embrace you," she replies.

So what, am I surrounded by hypocrites? Sim knows that her uncle told my aunt he doesn't want me anywhere around his niece. He's just mad that I'm beating him at his own game. He thinks he can use my aunt for money and get away with it. He must be out of his mind. Still, I've fallen for Sim, and losing her without a replacement isn't something I can do right now.

"Well, how am I supposed to see you if our relationship is supposed to be a secret?"

"Our parents would kill us if they found out we were sneaking around making out in dark corners. I'm running out of excuses to tell my parents, and with homework, social clubs, and sports training starting, I won't have much time for a relationship," she says. "I'm sorry!"

All I hear is excuses. Why does it feel like I'm the only one trying to make things work?

Romero is silent. Simone starts crying.

"Do you have anything to say?" asks Simone.

Maybe I can get my cousin to ask her to visit and then go over to my cousin's house. That is how we met after all. We can go back to basics on as many weekends as we can until

I get my licence. Then I'll borrow my parents' car and see her when they're sleeping. Yeah, that seems doable for now.

Before allowing Romero the opportunity to speak, she interrupts his thoughts. "I still want to be friends."

Oh my gosh, she's breaking up with me. This whole conversation was a setup for a breakup.

"I don't know what to say, Sim. It feels like my heart has been shattered into a thousand pieces," says Romero. "What happened to us one day getting married and you having my kids? Or was that a lie?"

"I still want those things one day. I just have to focus on preparing for it until the time comes. Please don't hate me, I do love you," says Simone.

Romero's mother picks up the phone and starts dialling. *Not again.*

"Hello?" says Romero's mom. Simone giggles.

I can't wait to move out of this house.

"Mom, I'm on the phone."

"Boy, hurry up and get off the phone. You've been on there for hours. You need to spend more time studying your schoolwork and stop talking to these fast girls."

Romero rolls his eyes. "Sim, I got to go. I'll call you later."

"Who is this Sim that is on the phone?" asks his mother.

"She's a friend, Mom," answers Romero.

"Mmhmm, I hope y'all studying your schoolwork,"

his mother says firmly. "You better not be bringing home any children in this house."

Simone continues to giggle. His mother hangs up.

"Ugh, that was so embarrassing."

"See, your mother basically confirmed us breaking up is for the best," says Simone.

"I know, it's just spending last summer with you was the best time of my life, and I want all of my remaining days on this Earth to be like last summer," says Romero.

"Awww, you're so sweet. You're not making this easy," says Simone.

"That's why you should reconsider us breaking up," says Romero optimistically. "Anyway, I got to let you go before my mother picks up the phone and kills me with embarrassment again."

Romero's mother picks up the phone again and starts pressing buttons. He exhales deeply and then hangs up.

Today is the worst day of my life.

"ROMERO?"

"YES, MOM?"

He stands to his feet and exits the room. He walks toward the kitchen and sees his mother in an apron watching television from the kitchen. The news is on, and it's covering the shooting that took place at the school earlier.

"Why didn't you tell me about the shooting that happened at school?"

Why, so you can have something additional to gossip to your sisters about?

"I tried to tell you when I got in from school, but you were on the phone talking to Aunty Crystal."

"Do you know who did it?"

"I didn't see what happened. All I heard was gunshots and saw people running. That's also what I told the police."

"You spoke to the police without a parent or a lawyer present?"

If I tried to advocate for myself, you would have been angry because the school called you and interrupted your day, and you know we ain't got no money for a lawyer. I was doing our family a favour.

"Our principal said it's best that we cooperate with the police to help them out with their investigation."

"I don't like that at all, Romero. You're a minor. You should not be speaking to the police without a lawyer or a parent present," says his mother. "You don't see how the police are killing us Black folk for nothing these days."

There's just no winning in this house.

"Well, what am I supposed to do? It's not like I have the support of my teachers or principals. They'll look at me as being difficult, and then I'll get in trouble. If I get in trouble with them, they'll call you, and you'll beat me when I get home. It's a lose-lose situation."

"Well, I'm just happy you haven't been hurt," says his mother.

"Hey, Mom, I overheard a few kids were going to therapy to process the potential trauma from what happened at school today. Do you think that's something that I can do?"

"Chile, therapy is a scam. I'm not paying another person to talk to you about your problems. Besides, you didn't get shot, you don't have any bills, and you don't have a job, so what can you possibly be stressed about?" asks his mother.

Why do I even bother trying?

CHAPTER 9
HOW ABOUT WE PLAY FOR IT?

Back at the apartment, Thomas and Desmond are in the bathroom with the door locked. They are playing a YouTube video on how to fix toilets. Thomas lifts the cover and sees the chain is broken in the toilet bowl. He pulls the chain from the bottom of the bowl and shows Desmond.

"Shit, what are we going to do now?" asks Desmond.

"We can get the superintendent to replace the toilet in the morning, but for now we'll have to manually flush by lifting this thing up," answers Thomas, pointing to the toilet flapper.

"Ewww, I'm not putting my hand in that dirty water. That's nasty," replies Desmond.

Thomas shakes his head and laughs. "What difference does it make? You're going to wash your hands anyway," he explains sarcastically. "Besides, us getting our hands dirty in this water doesn't solve the bigger problem."

Thomas pulls the gun out of the toilet bowl. "We gotta find a new spot for this gun."

"We might need to be like Lil Wayne and sleep with it under our pillow," suggests Desmond.

"And what if it accidentally goes off and kills one of us?" asks Thomas facetiously. "We got an even bigger problem. We can't keep the gun in here. If my mom finds out, she'll say I'm a bad influence on you, and then you'll have to find a new place to live," he adds.

Desmond paces back and forth. "I don't give a damn. I'm not going back to Jamaica. How about we keep it in our bags for now?"

Thomas looks at Desmond like he's crazy. "Keep it in our bags? Are you stupid? She packs our lunches every morning. We need to get rid of this thing now."

Brenda knocks on the bathroom door. "How are things coming in there? Did you guys fix it yet?"

"Still working on it, Mom," answers Thomas. "Fuck man, we're running out of time. We can't keep stalling in here, we're going to look suspicious," he whispers.

"Look, man, we don't have any other choice. We'll put it in our school bags for now and hide it in our rooms until we can figure something out," says Desmond.

"I want this gun out of my house before we sleep," demands Thomas.

"What about Romero? We had his back with John. Maybe he'll hold on to it as a way of paying us back," suggests Desmond.

"I don't know, man, that's a lot to ask someone you just met, even with us saving him from John. But the less people we have involved, the better," says Thomas.

"But how do we convince him to keep the gun until Kalinda comes back for it?" asks Desmond.

"Let's hope he won't have to have it for that long."

"All right, I'll message him on the 'gram," says Desmond.

He pulls out his phone and starts messaging Romero: *We need to meet tonight.*

"What do we do in the meantime?" asks Desmond.

He looks over to the gun. Thomas dries the gun, takes out the clip, and puts it in his underwear.

Desmond starts laughing. He points to the wet spot on Thomas's pants.

"Aside from looking like you pissed yourself, now you look bigger," says Desmond, laughing. Thomas rolls his eyes and shakes his head, then turns the doorknob. Brenda sits on the chair, acting as if she has been there the whole time, waiting.

"Shut up, you idiot," says Thomas, holding the door open.

Desmond laughs on his way out of the bathroom.

"Did you guys fix it?" asks Brenda.

"We need a chain. We can buy a new one from the dollar store, or we could have the super replace it for free, up to you. I'm easy either way," says Thomas with a smile.

His mother looks at him suspiciously. "Easy, eh? We can let the superintendent deal with it in the morning. I don't want you guys to leave the house for the rest of the night."

Thomas and Desmond look at each other nervously then look back at Brenda. "Yes ma'am," they say before walking back to their room.

Inside the room, Desmond turns on the television and PlayStation. He sits on the bed, waiting for the game to start, and then hands Thomas a controller.

"You game?" asks Desmond.

Thomas hesitates at first. "Fuck it, I need the distraction," he says, grabbing the controller. "Who you picking?" he asks, navigating through teams.

Desmond selects the Lakers, nodding to the beat of the music playing in the background.

Desmond gets a notification on his phone. He unlocks his phone and sees a message from Romero. Desmond reads the text out loud. "*I can't. My mother won't let me out of the house on a school night. We're dealing with a child who has a bedtime.*"

"One of us should stay back to keep my mom from being suspicious," says Thomas.

"One of us? Don't you mean you?" asks Desmond.

"You probably have a better excuse than me. After all, you actually know him," says Thomas.

"Know him? I barely had a day with him. I've basically spent the same amount of time with him as you," says Desmond.

Desmond's player steals the ball from Thomas's player and dunks it. He stands to his feet, dancing and showboating. Thomas has his player quickly inbound the ball and shoot a three. He misses, catches the rebound, but Desmond's player blocks his player when he tries to dunk it.

"GET OUT!" yells Desmond.

Thomas narrows his eyes at Desmond, who capitalizes on the turnover, bringing the ball up with his player. But Thomas's player quickly steals the ball and shoots a three-pointer — it goes in. He puts his finger to his lips. "Ssshhhhh," says Thomas as he laughs.

"How about we play for it?" suggests Desmond. "If I win, you have to go and drop off the gun to Romero, and if you win, I have to go."

"Deal, but first ask if we can come over," asks Thomas.

Desmond pauses the game and DMs Romero. He puts his phone down, awaiting a response. Thomas unpauses the game and steals the ball from Desmond, who quickly grabs his controller but doesn't recover fast enough.

Thomas shoots another three. He's up by one point. Desmond inbounds the ball, and Thomas's team defends with a full-court press. Desmond performs a series of crossovers on Thomas's players and drives to the basket. Thomas issues a double-teams as Desmond's player gets in the key, forcing a turnover. The buzzer goes off.

Thomas stands to his feet with his hands in the air, holding up an imaginary belt.

"Yo, that wasn't fair, I wasn't ready!" says Desmond.

"If you were at a disadvantage, you wouldn't have continued playing," says Thomas.

"Yo, you're wrong for that. God knows you're wrong for that, but whatever, deal's a deal," says Desmond.

"What's your excuse to leave the house gonna be?"

"Going to tell Aunty Brenda that I gotta get a textbook from a friend, or I won't be able to do my homework."

"Damn, that's a good lie, and you guys are in the same class, so everything lines up," says Thomas, embracing Desmond.

"Is that the gun I feel, or are you just really happy?" teases Desmond.

Thomas releases the hug and gives Desmond a shove before lifting up his shirt, revealing the gun with an unenthusiastic look. Desmond continues to laugh.

"It's okay. I won't tell anyone about your feelings for me," says Desmond.

"Shut up," says Thomas.

"Pass me my backpack. I want to get this over with so I can catch the exhibition match on Roku."

Thomas passes the bag over to Desmond. He takes out the gun from his underwear and clip from his pocket and hands them to Desmond. Desmond makes a disgusted face.

"At least wipe it, you'd think you'd know better with us living together and being cousins."

"Shut up, man. You talk so much shit," says Thomas.

"It's all good when it's jokes, but when I call you out it's a problem, huh?" asks Desmond sarcastically.

Thomas guides him to the door.

"Talk about a push. This is the only time you've ever pushed me to do anything, now that I've thought about it."

"If you don't want to do it, just say you don't want to do it, and then I'll do it myself, because I can't with the back and forth. You're driving me crazy," says Thomas.

Desmond starts taking off the bag.

"So you were doing it on purpose? Hell nah," says Thomas. "Look, I actually think your excuse is more valid than mine, and you're our best shot at getting this to him. Plus, remember this keeps you from going back to Jamaica," says Thomas.

"You're right. I got this," says Desmond, throwing the backpack over his shoulder.

Thomas escorts Desmond out of the room and into the living room. Brenda is sitting on the couch laughing at a sitcom.

"She looks happy," says Desmond.

Desmond takes a step forward, but Thomas holds him back.

"We should probably wait until a commercial comes on."

CHAPTER 10
NO ONE WOULD BOTHER LOOKING IN THERE

A commercial for Colgate comes on. Brenda puts it on mute, awaiting an explanation for Desmond and Thomas's interruption.

"Can I help you boys?"

Desmond starts walking in the opposite direction. Thomas turns him around.

"I forgot my textbook at school," says Desmond.

"Oh, and what do you want me to do about that?" asks Brenda.

"One of my classmates is willing to let me use his textbook if I come to his house now," says Desmond nervously. "Is it okay for me to walk over there, pick it up, and bring it back?"

Brenda ponders for a moment before answering.

"Thomas, go with him and make sure he comes back safely."

"Yes, Mom," answers Thomas.

Thomas and Desmond put on their shoes and exit the house. They strike victory poses at the elevator.

"I didn't know that my plan would work so good," says Thomas.

"*Your* plan? Don't you mean *my* plan?"

"It doesn't matter whose plan it is. All that matters is the execution."

"Okay, so we walking or are we taking the bus?" asks Desmond.

"Let's take the bus. That way we'll make it back ahead of time. I don't want to give my mom a reason to yell at me," says Thomas.

Desmond points to the 45 Kipling northbound bus in the distance. The boys run as fast as they can to the bus stop at Kipling and Rexdale but the bus is not in service. They throw up their hands in frustration as it drives past. Thomas checks the schedule, then looks at his watch.

"The next bus should be here in fifteen minutes. We still got time," says Thomas.

The boys sit inside the bus shelter. Desmond pulls out his phone and starts scrolling through social media. He checks Kalinda's Instagram story. The story is a picture of Kalinda wearing a ski mask and a sports bra. The caption reads *no face no case*, and she is giving trigger fingers. Desmond turns his phone to show Thomas. He grabs the phone and looks at the photo.

"This bitch is going to get us in trouble," says Thomas angrily.

Desmond starts breathing heavily. Thomas walks over to him and holds him by the shoulders.

"Don't worry, you're not going back to Jamaica, I can promise you that. Bro, I don't understand how she can put a post up like that. Is she dumb?"

A bus that reads 45 N Kipling arrives and stops in front of the boys. They walk onto the bus and pay their fare. Thomas looks at the time on his phone. "It's only nine; we're still making good time."

Four stops later, the bus stops at a Tim Hortons. The driver exits and walks into the restaurant.

"Are you serious? I can't believe this is happening right now," says Thomas. "Out of all the time he needs to go on a break he chooses now, cha man."

"Bro, we should have never taken the Glock. This isn't worth all this stress. All I want to do is play ball. We shouldn't be worried about being deported or going to jail," says Desmond.

"Don't worry, cuzzo, we'll make it to Romero, he'll hide the Glock somewhere, and no one will ever look until Kalinda comes back looking for it," says Thomas.

The bus driver gets on the bus, closes the door, and drives off. After a couple of seconds, he again opens the doors.

"What is it now?" says Desmond.

He gets up and looks out the window. He sees an elderly woman walking slowly to the bus. Desmond pretends to shoot himself in the head repeatedly as the woman takes her time getting on.

Finally the bus drives off. Moments later, Thomas and Desmond exit the bus. Desmond looks at his phone, verifying the address.

"Well, this must be it — 2173 Kipling Avenue," Desmond says.

They walk up to the door. Desmond knocks. Romero's mother opens the door wearing a bathrobe with her hair in curlers.

"I'm sorry, boys, we're not interested in buying anything tonight," she says, closing the door before Thomas or Desmond have a chance to speak.

"Are you sure this is the right house?" asks Thomas, knocking on the door again.

This time Romero opens the door.

***

Looks like we're still cool. I wonder why they're here, he thinks.

Thomas and Desmond are pleasantly surprised when Romero opens the door.

"What's up, guys?" asks Romero.

Thomas looks behind Romero and sees his younger brother Leonard holding a toy replica of the gun. Thomas's and Leonard's eyes meet.

"Is there somewhere we can go that's private?" asks Thomas.

Romero looks behind him and sees Leonard looking back and forth between Thomas and his Nintendo Switch.

This is why I can't have any friends. I have no privacy. You know what, I'm just going to act cool.

"Yeah," says Romero as he closes the door and leads Thomas and Desmond to the back of the house. "Right this way."

Romero sits on the steps of the deck. "So, what's up?"

Desmond flashes the gun from the backpack. Romero backs away.

Why did they bring that here? Are they crazy? I hope they're not going to kill me for not taking the gun when Kalinda asked me to take it earlier. I hope they aren't going to ask me to hold on to it.

Thomas puts his hands up. "It's okay we're not here to hurt you. We came to ask for a favour."

Here goes...

"What kind of favour?" asks Romero nervously.

"We need you to hide this until Kalinda comes back looking for it," asks Desmond.

"WHAT! ARE YOU FUCKING CRAZY?" yells Romero.

Thomas gestures with his hands for Romero to lower his voice.

"Sorry," whispers Romero. "My mother would kick me out of the house if she found out that I had a gun here. I got three younger brothers, and they're all nosy. If she doesn't find it, one of them will, and they'll show her just to watch me get an ass whooping."

"Please, bro, we got no one else to turn to, and the only reason we came all this way is because we remembered how grateful you were when we saved you from John," answers Desmond.

Romero ponders for a moment and thinks about John beating him up if Thomas and Desmond hadn't been there. They were there for him with John. They also looked out for him in the cafeteria. This could be his chance to earn their respect and get back good with Kalinda.

"Okay, fine. I'll do it," he says. "But only for tonight. I'm bringing it to school tomorrow and handing it back to her, whether she has a plan or not," says Romero.

"Fine by us," answer Thomas and Desmond in unison.

"Oh, by the way, do you have a textbook?" asks Desmond.

"We never got textbooks today, remember?"

"Shit, you're right," says Desmond with a worried look.

"What's wrong?" Romero asks.

"That was my excuse for getting out of the house."

"Damn, what's going to happen if you show up empty-handed?" asks Romero.

"Let's just say Thomas and I will be sore at school tomorrow," says Desmond.

They share a laugh. Thomas takes the gun out of the backpack and hands it to Romero. Romero pushes the gun back at him.

"I can't just walk in the house with a gun," he says.

"Put it in your underwear," suggests Thomas.

Desmond makes a disgusted face and chuckles to himself. Romero observes Desmond's reaction and hesitates to take the gun.

"Be careful — that's where he had it before we got here," says Desmond.

"Uh-uh, that's like having our dicks touch through the gun! I don't think so," says Romero.

Romero and Desmond laugh while Thomas shakes his head.

"How about your socks?" suggests Desmond.

Romero grabs the gun from Thomas and puts it in his sock. He takes a couple of steps around the backyard. "Okay I think it's secure."

"Aight, I'll see y'all at school tomorrow," he says, doing handshakes with Thomas and Desmond.

Desmond and Thomas give Romero the deuce just before running to the bus stop. Romero looks back to watch them get on. Once the bus drives off, he steps inside the house. His stepfather is passed out in the chair, holding an empty bottle of beer in front of the television while highlights from the basketball game play.

Romero tiptoes through the living room, turns off the television. He walks through the kitchen and to the basement, looking for a place to stash the gun. His eyes land on the furnace room, and he smiles.

No one would bother looking in there.

He takes out the electrical tape he spots in his stepfather's toolbox then walks into the furnace room. He tapes the gun to the back of the furnace and then checks to see if it's secure. On his way out of the furnace room, his eyes meet with Leonard at the basement stairs.

CHAPTER 11
YOU WOULDN'T BELIEVE ME IF I TOLD YOU

Leonard stands at the middle of the stairway, smiling, pointing his toy gun at Romero.

"Ugh, why are you always around?" asks Romero.

"Mom said it's time for bed," he says.

"I'm coming. I was just putting away my laundry," responds Romero.

Romero quickly walks toward the stairs, guiding Leonard back up with his hands. Leonard hesitates as he continues to look at the furnace.

"Come on, you said it's time to go to bed, so lead the way." He continues to rush Leonard upstairs.

A distracted Leonard missteps and falls on the stairs.

"Ouch!"

"Ugh," exclaims Romero, rolling his eyes.

Romero's mother comes to the top of the stairs. "What's all this commotion about?"

Romero's anxiety increases. "Leonard fell on our way up the stairs."

"Why are y'all in the basement?"

"I was looking for something in the laundry, and Leonard came down to get me," answers Romero. "Are you okay, Leonard?"

Leonard nods, stands, and limps up the stairs.

When Leonard gets to the top, their mother comforts him on the way to the bedroom. Leonard lies on the bottom bunk, and his mother tucks him in. She takes the toy gun from his hand and puts it on the top of the dresser.

"I hate that you play with this thing!" she says.

Romero climbs up to the top bunk, almost hitting his head as he crawls onto the bed. He lies down.

I hate that I have to sleep up here. I should be the one that sleeps on the bottom bunk. I hate this stupid house and its stupid rules.

Their mother switches off the light. After a few moments, Leonard is fast asleep and snoring. Romero tosses and turns in bed, pushing his pillows against his ears, trying to muffle the sound.

Ugh, I wish I had my own room. How am I going to get any rest under these conditions? Not that I could sleep anyway.

Continuing to cover his ears with the pillows, he imagines getting caught at school with the gun and going to jail.

He quietly sneaks out of bed and walks to the living room, looking for the wireless house phone in the dark, wondering if Sim is still up.

He uses the streetlights that shine into the house from the window to guide him to the phone stand.

"There it is," he whispers.

He picks up the phone and then glances at the clock in the kitchen stove. He hesitates for a moment before dialling.

"Hello?" Simone whispers.

Romero lowers the volume, then looks down the hallway to see if anyone is coming. He gets up and walks down to the basement, closing the door behind him.

"Hey," he whispers. "Look, I know you said you want things to be over, but I really need you right now."

"What's wrong?"

"You won't believe me if I told you, but I have a gun."

"A gun? Why?"

"I can't go into all of the details, but there was a shooting at my school and I'm helping a friend keep a low profile."

"What if the police find the gun in your possession and arrest you?"

"I only have to keep the gun hidden for twenty-four hours."

"Then what?"

"Then I give the gun back and go back to my life," Romero answers.

Romero knows that "back to my life" includes the respect and support of Desmond and Thomas. He doesn't have much of an attachment to Kalinda, so if she disappears with the gun, he's at peace with it.

"I think you should turn your friend into the authorities," says Simone.

He pictures himself getting beat up by Jamarcus, Latrell, and Kalinda.

"Haven't you heard, Sim? Snitches get stitches. Turning anyone in is a death wish, and besides, I can't comment on what happened because I wasn't there. All I know is that it was an accident."

"If it was an accident, why can't your friend just explain that to the police?"

Romero feels that the police wouldn't believe his friend. He has heard the stories from the States about how the police treat Black people, and he fears the same fate. He pictures different scenarios in which police are assaulting him, planting drugs on him, shooting him, and putting him in prison.

"Maybe it's because you're half white, or maybe it's the little bougie neighbourhood you live in, but the cops around here shoot first, then ask questions last," says Romero. "A couple of years ago a kid lost an eye to a couple of off-duty cops. The family still hasn't gotten justice."

He thinks back to the story of Dafonte Miller, when two off-duty cops assaulted him, causing him to lose one of his eyes.

"Me being half-white has nothing to do with my Black experience," explains Simone.

Sim is half Ukrainian and half Jamaican. She has silky hair, green eyes, and a body like Rihanna. She runs track and field and is also in the gifted program. Romero thinks of her as his meal ticket. He just knows she's going to make something out of herself one day, and he wants to be the man in her corner when it all happens.

After getting to know her both intimately and emotionally, Romero grew fond of her. The more time they spent over the summer, the more his feelings grew, until he accidentally said the words "I love you." He lost all power when he said those words, and he knew it. He hoped Sim's heart was pure enough that she wouldn't take advantage.

"Um, Sim, I love you, but please don't give me that bullshit. If you can't recognize your privilege, then we have another problem," says Romero.

"How could you—"

"—You know, I called you to get support. I was hoping you'd have my back or give me words of encouragement, but all you're doing is creating doubt, and I don't need that right now," he interrupts.

"You know what, if you're going to throw your life away for someone you probably barely even know, then I'm happy I ended things with you," says Simone.

"I don't need this shit," says Romero. He hangs up the phone and exhales deeply. He stands to his feet and puts the phone back on the charger, stubbing his toe against the furniture. "Fuck," he whispers, quietly limping back to his room.

He struggles to use the stairs because of the pain in his toe. He eventually loses his balance, and falls. He brings himself to his feet and stumbles up the stairs to the kitchen. His mother gets out of bed and enters the kitchen, turns the light on.

"Why are you making so much noise?"

"I'm sorry, I hurt my toe on the way out of the kitchen getting some water," says Romero.

"Be more careful next time. Troy has to get up early in the morning."

She shuts off the light and goes back to her room.

Romero goes to his room. After climbing up on his bed, he lies restlessly replaying the argument with Simone until finally falling asleep.

CHAPTER 12
THEY'RE COMING FOR ME

Hours later the alarm clock goes off. BEEP! BEEP!

Romero carefully crawls out of bed and down the bunk bed stairs. He walks into the bathroom, yawning and rubbing his eyes. He grabs the toothpaste and sees that it's almost finished.

I'm so tired of this ghetto shit.

He grabs the scissors, cuts open the tube, and scrapes the inside with a toothbrush. He turns on the water and wets the toothbrush before brushing his teeth. After rinsing and flossing, he undresses. He turns the shower on and enters. He presses play from an old boombox that sits on the toilet. Within minutes the bathroom is filled with steam. He skips songs until "Loyal To A Fault" by Big Sean comes on. Romero sings to the lyrics while lathering and rinsing.

There is banging on the door.

"Rome, you're going to waste all the hot water. This is no time for a concert. Soap, rinse your skin, and get out," his mother says in her Guyanese accent.

I can't even grieve this breakup in peace!

He quickly rinses off the remaining soap, shuts off the music, wraps a towel around himself, and rushes out of the bathroom. His mother shakes her head at him as she sees him rush out.

Romero lotions his skin and then quickly puts on his uniform. He peeks out of his room, looking for his mother's location. He sees his parents' door slightly open and overhears them arguing.

"The only reason we're behind on our bills is because you stuck your dick in that bitch and had a kid with her," says his mother angrily.

Oh, look, they're distracted. This is the perfect opportunity for me to retrieve the gun without detection.

As he walks out of the room, Leonard gets up, grabs his toy gun from the dresser, and follows Romero into the basement. He trails behind slightly, watching Romero go down the basement stairs.

Once Romero is in the basement, he tears the tape off the gun and ammo clip from the furnace. He puts the clip in the gun and puts it in his backpack.

"Romero," yells his mother.

He jumps, startled.

He sighs before answering. "YES, MOM?"

"I NEED YOU TO HELP ME GET THESE KIDS READY FOR SCHOOL!" she yells.

He rushes up the stairs, leaving his backpack on the floor next to the back-door exit.

He crosses paths with Leonard on his way to his eight-year-old brother Lamarques and four-year-old brother Lamar's room.

"All right, guys, let's get you ready," Romero says.

He goes into their closet and pulls out shirts and pants for them to wear, then hands Lamarques his clothes.

"If you can get dressed on your own, I'll get you a cookie," he says, handing him a shirt and a pair of jeans. He holds his pants open for him to put his leg in one at a time.

"Make that two cookies and we got a deal," says Lamarques.

Romero rolls his eyes. "Fine, two cookies."

Romero exits the room. Before walking into his parents' bedroom, he sees Leonard holding his toy gun, zipping his backpack. Romero bolts across the hall to Leonard, snatching the bag out of his hand. He looks inside the bag, confirming the gun is still there…

"Are you fucking stupid? Why are you going through my stuff?"

Leonard holds the gun up to his brother. His mother and stepfather observe him talking harshly to Leonard.

His stepfather walks into the kitchen. "Who the fuck are you to talk to my son that way?"

Romero looks to his mother, expecting her to defend him.

You guys are such hypocrites.

"Michelle, talk to your son, because if he ever talks to my son that way again I'll bust open his mouth," he says.

So much for being one big happy family. I'm out.

He wipes the tears from his eyes as he grabs his school bag and storms out of the house. He walks into the school with his fists clenched, looking through the halls for Desmond and Thomas.

I got to get rid of this thing.

The bell rings before he can locate them. He walks to his homeroom class and sees Desmond sitting at the back of the class with Broach. He salutes them, then finds his seat next to Katrina. She grabs his wrist.

"Did you hear what happened yesterday with that Latino kid?" asks Katrina.

Romero looks back at Desmond, verifying whether or not he heard. He locks eyes with Desmond and nods.

Remember, you weren't there, so you didn't see what happened.

He looks back at Katrina. "Nah, I was in the cafeteria, but aside from hearing the shots fired, I didn't see anything."

An announcement comes over the classroom speaker: "The level of cooperation the police received from our students yesterday hasn't been helpful in their investigation. As a result, the police will be going through lockers and students' backpacks in search of the fireman that was discharged in the cafeteria during lunch yesterday."

"That's a violation of our rights," says one of the white students in the class.

"They should just search the lockers of the people they suspect," says another white student.

Romero gets up from his seat and walks to the back of the class; he taps Desmond on the shoulder and walks farther back.

Desmond gets up from his seat and stands alongside Romero. He points to the white students that were talking earlier.

"Can you believe that shit, man?"

"Believe what?" asks Romero.

"It's a violation of our rights!" mocks Desmond.

Romero chuckles at the impersonation. "That's just their privilege speaking. They don't know that this is routine for us."

Romero hadn't come in contact with police at the other school, except during their D.A.R.E. program. Instead of getting any attention from the police officer, he was ignored. But he'd heard stories from his older cousins and pretended to understand, as though he had experienced it.

"Anyway, what's gwanning?"

Desmond leans in to whisper into Romero's ear: "You bring the heat?"

"That's what I wanted to talk to you about. The boi dem are here checking lockers and bags, and I have it in my bag," whispers Romero. "What am I supposed to do?"

"Dunno man, you gotta stash it somewhere before you get sucked," says Desmond.

"But where?" asks Romero nervously.

"First thing we did when we got home last night was put it in the toilet bowl," says Desmond. "I think based on time, that's your best option."

Desmond shrugs and then walks back to his desk to sit.

Romero visualizes going into the bathroom stall and stashing the gun inside the toilet bowl.

He exhales deeply and walks back to his desk. He grabs his backpack and puts it over his shoulder, heading for the exit.

"Are you okay?" asks Mr. Logan.

Romero turns around, holds his stomach, and looks at him. "I'll be fine, just need to go to the bathroom."

Mr. Logan makes a face and gestures for Romero to leave.

He walks out of the room and sees police officers opening lockers and searching through them.

Shit, they're so close!

He speed-walks pass them, avoiding detection as they

search a student's locker. He enters the boys' bathroom, looking frantically for an empty stall. He finds the last door is open. He enters the stall, locks the door, and rolls up his sleeves to place the gun inside the toilet tank, accidentally breaking the chain. He puts his backpack over his shoulder and puts the lid back on the toilet. He unlocks the doors and walks out of the stall. He washes his hands and exits.

The police see Romero exit the bathroom with his backpack. They make eye contact before Romero breaks eye contact and walks back to class.

"Hey," says a police officer, trying to get Romero's attention.

He ignores the police and continues to walk but increases his pace. He feels anxious.

They're probably calling another kid.

The police officers increase their pace too. Romero quickly looks back. He sees them catching up.

Shit, they're coming for me. He starts remembering images from the viral murder of George Floyd, where the officer held his knee over his neck. He's scared.

He starts to run. They chase after him, tackle him to ground, and pin his arm behind his back while putting their knees to the back of his neck.

He screams loudly as he gasps for air.

Is this how I'm going to die? he thinks as the officer's knee is pushed against his neck.

His classmates gather at the door with their cellphones out, recording the interaction. One of the officers grabs his backpack, unzips it, and empties everything onto the floor while the other moves his knee from his neck to his back. Romero begins coughing after finally being able to breathe. The officer holding the backpack redirects the students in the hallway with their cameras out.

"All right, keep it moving. There's nothing to see," says the officer.

After thoroughly going through the backpack, there's no gun. The officer looks up to his partner.

"There's nothing in here."

The officer picks up Romero's books and puts them back in the bag. The other officer stands and brings Romero up from the floor. He hands him his backpack then dusts off his uniform.

"Sorry, kid, you shouldn't have run. You looked suspicious. At least you're innocent, no harm, no foul," says the officer.

Romero is shaking like a leaf, still processing what happened. He holds his bag and stands against the wall, watching the officers continue the search as if he hadn't just been traumatized.

He tries to zip the bag up but sees the zipper is broken. He stands still, and then tears start to roll down his cheek. He wipes the tears from his eyes and looks around at all the students filming him and judging him.

He continues to replay being tackled by the police in his mind. He loosens his collar and touches his neck, remembering what it felt like to be without air.

John walks down the hall with his crew. They point at Romero, who is wiping tears from his face.

"Look at this pussy crying," says John, and his friends join in, pointing and laughing at Romero before he runs out of the school.

CHAPTER 13
HAVEN'T I BEEN THROUGH ENOUGH?

Romero sits on the steps of the stairs that lead to the teachers' parking lot.

The bell rings. A crowd of students come out of the building and surround him.

"Yo, are you the kid that fought those cops in the hallway?" asks a student.

"Oh my gosh, are you okay?" asks Desiree.

"Did they hurt you?" asks Katrina.

So it took being tackled by the police to get all this extra attention? I can get used to this.

Desiree manoeuvres to the other side of Romero and rests her hands on his shoulder.

"Those cops are pussies for beating up on you like that," she says.

John and his crew observe the attention Romero is getting from a distance and scoff to themselves. Thomas, Desmond, and Broach come out of the building looking for Romero. Broach spots him, extends his arm to shake hands.

"Yo, forget the boi dem. Them pigs can't mess with my man Romero," he says.

Broach puts his arm around Romero, and the crowd cheers.

Mr. Da Vinci comes out of the school and looks at Romero in the crowd. "All right everyone, back to class." Then he calls Romero over with his finger.

Unsure if Mr. Da Vinci is pointing to him, he looks around and then back at Mr. Da Vinci. He points to his chest. Mr. Da Vinci nods. Romero walks over; Broach, Thomas, and Desmond follow. Mr. Da Vinci locks eyes with each of the boys one by one, until landing on Romero.

"Everything all right?" asks Mr. Da Vinci.

He nods nervously. "I need you to sign some forms about what happened with you and the police officers."

"My homie Romero isn't signing anything or saying anything until he can speak to his parents about what happened," says Broach protectively.

Romero looks over to Broach with a smile. He looks over at Thomas and Desmond, feeling secure that they have his back.

"Don't make this out to be bigger than it actually is," says Mr. Da Vinci.

"Bigger? How would you like it if you got tackled by a couple of cops?" asks Broach. "If that happened to you, it would be all over the news in a heartbeat. Must be nice to have that complexion for your protection."

"Ooohhhh!" cheer Thomas and Desmond.

"Mr. Da Vinci got served," says Thomas.

The boys laugh and cheer as Mr. Da Vinci looks off.

"All right, get back to class."

The boys head for the entrance.

"Don't forget to see me before you go home today about those forms," Mr. Da Vinci reminds Romero with a smile.

Romero nods shyly and continues walking.

He doesn't care about me; he just wants to protect the reputation of the school and avoid a lawsuit.

Romero and Desmond walk into a noisy class of students huddled in groups. The class goes quiet and stares at Romero as he takes his seat. After a moment of awkward silence, a student blurts out:

"I heard you were holding a piece, and that's why they tackled you!"

"Bro, what's wrong with you? You Black, you should know better than to talk like that. You know all of our phones are tapped," responds Desmond.

He shakes his head and grips Romero's shoulder. He looks him in the face and points with his free hand.

"Don't say anything to anyone! No one gives a damn about you."

He looks around the room. "Especially none of these white kids."

Ms. Kowalski walks through the crowd of students and stops when she gets to Romero's desk.

"Can I speak to you for a minute?"

Romero exhales deeply, then gulps before standing up to his feet.

Haven't I been through enough? I hope this isn't about yesterday's assignment.

As he follows Ms. Kowalski to her desk, he looks around the room of students that stare at him as if he's on death row.

She whistles. "All right, everyone, back to your groups. Nothing to see here." The class reluctantly gets back to their groups. Romero looks around and sees he still has the attention of his peers.

"Don't pay any attention to them!"

He focuses on Ms. Kowalski's face.

"Are you okay?"

He nods.

"I heard about what happened earlier in the hallway."

He looks away, allowing his eyes to wander the classroom.

Can I please go back to my class and get this day over with?

"You poor thing!" She grabs his hand. He turns his attention back to her, making eye contact.

"If you ever need someone to talk to about what happened, or anything at all, you know where to find me," she continues. "I know things can be pretty tough for your people. If there's anything I can do to help or be there for you in any way, please let me know."

How would you know how tough things can be for my people? You're not Black, so how can you empathize? She's only taking the time to talk to me because of the rumours.

"Thank you. Is it okay if I go back to my desk now?"

"Yes, of course. I know you and your friend came in late, so you missed the instructions I gave to the class. We read an article and are now discussing the merits of the writer's argument. Have a quick read and join a group to get into a discussion. We'll discuss as a class tomorrow."

More work? Haven't I been through enough?

Romero walks back to his desk and starts reading the photocopied article left on his desk.

Desmond taps on his desk. "Everything okay?"

Romero takes his eyes off his paper and looks over to Desmond. "Yeah, she just wanted to ask me how I was doing. She was good until she started going off on how she knows things can be pretty tough for *your* people. As if she can relate to our struggles with her privileged ass."

Desmond chuckles.

"Yo, have you seen Kalinda?"

Desmond looks away and adjusts himself on his seat. "Nah!" He points to the clock. "But she has the same lunch as us, so we should see her soon."

The bell rings. Students quickly put their books away and rush to the doors. Romero and Desmond put away their books and wait for the class to empty. They stand as the last few students exit the class.

They open the hallway doors and walk through, accidentally bumping into Joel.

"Yo, I heard about what happened to you in the morning."

Romero avoids eye contact, nodding.

"That was messed up. I'm sorry about that, man."

"It's whatever, man!"

He daps Romero and embraces him. Romero wipes a tear and clears his throat.

"Please, Rome ain't let that phase him. We been let down, it's not like anyone cares."

Nick and Adrian notice Romero with Joel and Desmond.

"Bro, I heard what happened to you in the morning. Are you okay?"

"I guess you can rap about it now," says Nick, who nudges Adrian after making his joke. They chuckle.

"Does this kind of stuff happen to you guys a lot in your community?" asks Adrian.

Romero gives him a look.

"I live across the street from the school," says Romero, looking over to Desmond and JoJo.

"We just got to keep moving and find our allies," says Thomas.

Nick and Adrian look at each other after being intimidated by Thomas. They put up their fists in solidarity.

Desmond and JoJo laugh while mocking them. Romero steps aside, allowing Adrian and Nick to pass.

It doesn't look authentic the way you're holding up your fist. I wish these guys would understand me instead of trying to mimic what I do.

Thomas looks back, shaking his head at Nick and Adrian. He kisses his teeth and puts an arm around Romero.

"Don't worry about those guys. You're a G. If those guys were in your shoes, they would buckle under pressure."

Romero looks up to Thomas and smiles as they walk ahead of Desmond and JoJo. It feels good to be around people who understand.

When the boys enter the cafeteria, all goes quiet. People stop mid-chew, mid-sip, mid-bite, and the attention from the room moves to Romero. A bubble being blown from a student chewing gum pops. Romero gulps, turns his attention to the cafeteria lady, and gets in line for food. Whispers and murmurs fill the cafeteria as the line moves slowly.

The boys grab trays and hold them out to the cafeteria lady: mashed potatoes with lumpy gravy. John and his crew are at the back of the line, snickering.

Romero, Desmond, Thomas, and Broach grab their trays and find a table.

CHAPTER 14
WHERE THE F$&K IS THE GUN?

Inside a townhouse off John Garland Avenue, Kalinda is sitting on the couch watching television. A woman with a messy bun and gelled baby hairs comes down the stairs pulling down her top and buttoning up her jeans. She is followed by Kalinda's brother, Keith, who is twenty-one and sports a slim, muscular build. He wears his hair in braids and has covered his skin in tattoos.

He pulls down a ripped white tank top over his face and ties the strings of grey sweatpants before walking her to the door. He cracks it open and looks out before giving her a kiss. She walks out. He smiles before realizing the television is on in the living room. He pulls a gun from behind him that is tucked away in his pants.

He holds it out and canvasses the room before seeing Kalinda on the couch with her feet up, watching *Maury*.

Maury opens an envelope, pulls a paper out of it, and reads: "You are not the father." The woman on the television runs offstage, sobbing. The camera crew follows her.

Kalinda laughs hysterically. "Look at these loose-ass hoes just giving up the box and not even knowing who the daddy is."

Keith puts the safety on and taps the edge of the couch with his gun. "I don't remember seeing any PA days on the calendar."

A startled Kalinda sits up on the couch. "I ... wasn't feeling well, so I decided to stay home."

"You look fine to me."

"Yeah, well, it's my time of the month, you wouldn't understand."

"Wasn't it your time of the month last week?"

Kalinda looks at the gun in Keith's hand and begins to sweat. "Um, nah I was getting symptoms, but it didn't come."

"You need me to run to the store and get you something for the pain or some comfort snacks?"

"Nah, I'm good. I took a couple Advil an hour ago, and if I eat anymore ice cream, I'm going to throw up."

"Hmm, okay."

"New shorty?"

Keith chuckles. "Yeah, she studying political science

at York, and she works in the community centre running after-school programs for youth."

"Ooh, seems like a keeper."

"She's way out of my league. There ain't nothing I can do for her." Keith points to the surrounding area. "Just look at where we live. Look at our life."

Keith sits next to Kalinda on the couch. He places the gun on the table and leans back into the couch. She looks at the gun and then at him.

"What if she doesn't want anything from you? What if she's just getting to know you?"

"Doesn't want anything from me?" Keith laughs. "Everybody wants something. The only reason she's with me is so she can say that she tried to make a difference. She just looks at me as a hood project that she can run back to her friends and talk about. She don't really care about me."

"Then why even waste any time with her?"

"Have you seen her? She's hot. If I don't slide in another man will."

"Why does it need to be you, though?"

Keith shrugs. "Who knows, maybe she'll be our way out? Maybe she'll make it as a lawyer or a politician or something."

"Why would she want to be with a drug dealer if she's a lawyer or politician?"

"Politicians and lawyers are always doing business

with drug dealers, you just don't see it."

Kalinda gives Keith a surprised look.

"And you're not supposed to see it or hear about it, so don't ask," he adds.

"Have you ever thought about getting out of the game?"

"Out of the game? There ain't no getting out of the game for me, lil' sis. That road ended when our parents died. When I had to choose between a full scholarship to play ball and helping Nanna with you."

"You should have left."

"And let social services take you away after Nanna died? I don't think so. I heard what the foster care system does to kids, and it'll be a cold day in hell before I let anything happen to you."

"Yeah, but if you took the scholarship and played pro ball, then we wouldn't be living here."

"What if I took the scholarship and never made it to the pros? Then what?"

"I don't know. At least you tried."

"Trying isn't enough for people like us that get opportunities like that. We either make it or we don't. Once our parents died, it was either make guaranteed money on the streets or put my faith in a fantasy for kids. Besides, with Grandma not having no life insurance, it was an easy choice for me to make."

"I hate Fangs."

"Say what you want about Fangs, but if he hadn't

put me on, I would have lost you to social services and become homeless when Nanna died."

"There's got to be more to life than this."

"There is — for the privileged! But the system is set up so that people have to live this street life."

"Aren't you worried that you'll get killed or put in prison?"

"I'm just playing with the cards that I've been dealt. Trying to get better at bluffing. Once I put you through college, Imma find a way to get out of the game for good. But until then…"

Keith taps the gun on the table. "It's street life for me. Besides, if Mom and Dad weren't coming to my graduation the day of the accident, then they would still be alive."

"It's not your fault, Keith."

"Yeah, say what you want, sis, but if they never came to my graduation, they'd still be alive."

"No one blames you for that. You need to move on."

"You know, despite Nanna being sick, she told me to go to the States. She said I may never get another opportunity like this again. But I knew if she died taking care of you, I couldn't forgive myself."

"Yeah, but she died anyway."

"And if I never came back home, you probably would have ended up in foster care."

Kalinda sits up and hugs Keith. "Well, I'm glad you came home."

He hugs her back. Kalinda sits back on the couch and changes the channel.

"I hope you're smart enough," Keith says to Kalinda, "to know that everyone has a hidden agenda. You just got to figure out what it is before they accomplish it. Then you got to decide whether it aligns with what you want to do."

"Look who sounds all philosophical and shit!"

Keith laughs. "You really should spend more time reading books than watching *Maury* and other toxic shows that poorly represent Black people."

"What, you going to be a hypocrite and tell me to stop listening to rap music too?"

"Of course not. Those guys are poets telling you about how they cope with their PTSD and other mental health challenges. That's the only reason they winning awards. White people continue profiting off our trauma. People don't be winning for doing anything positive."

Kalinda starts counting on her hand. "What about the Nobel Peace Prize, humanitarian awards, lifetime achievements?"

"I guess you got a point."

"I mean, there are some good people in the world. You should give your shorty the benefit of the doubt. I mean, I'd want someone to give me the benefit of the doubt and not judge me according to my circumstance."

Keith nudges Kalinda. "You think you so smart, huh."

Kalinda giggles. "I don't like to brag, but you know."

Keith rolls his eyes. They share a laugh until Keith's eyes land on his gun on the table.

"You know, I was cleaning that today, and I realized that one of them was missing."

Keith picks the gun up from the table and clears a bullet from the chamber. "Would you happen to know anything about where it might have gone?"

Kalinda begins to sweat. She stands to her feet and paces. "Okay, so promise you won't get mad?"

Keith stands to his feet and gets in Kalinda's face. "Where the fuck is my strap?"

Kalinda backpedals. She holds her hands up, distancing herself from Keith.

"I borrowed it to scare some kids at school into giving me their lunch money."

"YOU DID WHAT? That's the stupidest thing I ever heard! Do you know what the police will do if they find that gun on you? THEY'LL FUCKING KILL YOU!"

Keith backhand slaps Kalinda.

She falls to the floor, and tears start rolling down her face. She wipes them with her hands before standing. Keith exhales deeply then puts his hand on his head and begins to pace.

"Where ... the fuck ... is the gun?"

"I don't know."

"*I don't know?* WHAT DO YOU MEAN YOU DON'T FUCKING KNOW?"

"I'm trying to explain!"

"Okay, explain."

"Things got out of control one day at lunch. Most kids either pay us or they give us an excuse for why they can't pay that day, and pay us the day after…"

Kalinda smirks, but Keith isn't impressed.

"Yesterday, this Spanish kid got brave. It was one thing for him to tell us that he didn't have any money, but this guy was just rude. He was like, *get the hell out of my way, I'm not paying*. He called us bums and told us to get jobs. We couldn't take any disrespect, so Jamarcus pulled the heat out on him."

Keith's eyes widen. "HE DID WHAT!"

"Jamarcus pulled the heat and the trigger went off in the scuffle … the kid took a flesh wound to the leg."

"Did the police come?"

"They did, but we escaped to McDonald's."

Keith sighs. "Okay, so where's the gun?"

"I gave it to one of my friends."

"You did *what*?"

"Don't worry, it's safe."

"Why did you give it to your friend instead of bring it home with you?"

"Jamarcus and Latrell got sucked by the boi dem."

"Those guys got caught?"

Kalinda nods. Keith shakes his head.

"There was nothing but squad cars all over the school.

I had to make a choice. I knew with my reputation that if I got sucked, I'd probably serve time, but the kids I gave it to are squeaky clean."

"Squeaky clean, eh?"

"These kids have never even seen detention."

"How do you know they won't crack under pressure?"

"Fear! They all fear me because of you and your reputation. They don't want to face your wrath."

"Kalinda, how could you be so stupid? If those kids snitch, the cops can trace that back to me, and then it's my ass that's in jail and your ass in the system."

Keith slaps Kalinda out of frustration, knocking her down to the floor.

"I'm sorry — I'm ... I'm just between the bills, and the guys—"

"—The boys I gave the strap to are at school now. I'll go now and pick it up."

Kalinda stands. Keith joins her.

"I'm coming."

"I don't know if that's necessary. I'll be in and out."

"I'm sure that's what you said the day you decided to hand my strap over to another man."

"I got to go to the bathroom real quick."

"Hurry up."

Kalinda rushes to the bathroom and locks the door. She takes a look in the mirror and touches her black eye with her hand.

She winces. She picks up a pair of sunglasses from the counter and a bandana. She puts the sunglasses on and ties the bandana around her face. She puts her hood up and walks out of the bathroom.

Keith sits in the kitchen, waiting. He looks up at Kalinda.

"You ready?"

"Let's go."

CHAPTER 15
TRUST ISSUES

JoJo joins Desmond, Romero, Thomas, and Broach at the table, holding a plate of curly fries. Desmond attempts to steal a fry. Joel pulls back and covers his food with his hand while chewing.

"Mans are going to be greedy?" asks Desmond.

"Mans haven't eaten anything for the day," JoJo scoffs.

"Fine!"

He unshields his food and extends the fries to Desmond.

"Have one!"

Desmond grabs a few and scarfs them down before JoJo can say anything. JoJo kisses his teeth.

"See, this is why mans have trust issues!"

Romero chuckles at the back and forth.

The bell rings and students begin exiting the cafeteria. JoJo crumbles up his garbage into a ball. He crosses over to the left and to the right, leaps into the arm…

And gets blocked by John. Losing his balance, he falls to the ground.

"Yo, that wasn't cool!" says Desmond, helping Joel up.

"Yeah? Do something about it."

Mr. Logan enters the cafeteria and walks over to the boys.

"You guys trying out for the basketball team after school?"

"Of course, somebody has to help Broach out there. We got people on the team that don't know how to use their height." Desmond looks at John, then back at Romero, and nudges him.

"Ooh, that sounded like a shot at you," says Mr. Logan, looking at John. John rolls his eyes.

"Don't listen to Brick City over there. This guy couldn't buy a shot, even if he had Elon money."

"Me? You can build a house with the amount of bricks you throw."

"Okay, calm down, that's enough. Save that energy for the court. Maybe this year the team will make the playoffs." Mr. Logan glances at the clock. "Why aren't you guys in class?"

The boys look away.

"Because we're talking to you."

"You know, sir, you're a bad example," says Romero with a smirk. They share a laugh. Mr. Logan wags his finger up and down while shaking his head.

"All right, you guys head to class."

Romero and Desmond tiptoe into History class. The teacher is writing on the chalkboard. They quietly pull out their chairs from their desks and have a seat. Romero exhales a sigh of relief.

"Nice of you to join us," says the teacher before turning around to pick up a clipboard from his desk. "Mr. Anthony and Mr. Samuels, I presume?"

Romero and Desmond look at each other, then back at Mr. Greene.

"How did he…"

"How do I know?"

"We're the only two new kids in the class," whispers Desmond.

"Would you like to tell the class why you skipped class yesterday?"

Romero looks at Desmond with sweat dripping down his face.

"Well, do you have anything to say for yourself?"

"It was personal, and it won't happen again," responds Desmond.

Romero looks at Desmond, surprised at his response. They quietly pull out their chairs from their desks. Romero exhales a sigh of relief.

"Pick your battles," he whispers.

Romero sits down and opens his backpack; his stomach begins to rumble. He raises his hand. Mr. Greene looks at him, annoyed.

"Yes?"

"May I be excused to go to the washroom?"

"Please be quick, I'm about to start the lesson."

Romero gets up and exits the class. On the way to the bathroom, he sees John and his crew standing in the hallways, beatboxing and rapping. Romero avoids eye contact and looks down as he walks past them. George is distracted by Romero and stops beatboxing. He steps away from the rap circle and taps Romero on the shoulder.

"Yo, so what's it like getting tackled and beat down by the boi dem?"

John and the rest of the crew circle Romero.

"Not so tough now without your cousins, are you?"

John pushes Romero's shoulder back. Romero narrows his eyes at John. He gets up into his face.

"What? You going to hit me?"

John pushes his shoulder back.

"Come on, hit me."

John pushes his shoulder back again.

"Come on, I want you to hit me."

I wonder if I hit him, will they jump in?

Romero looks at each of the boys in John's crew. He

throws a punch. John ducks, and the punch lands on George's face. Bryson, Victor, and John look at George before throwing punches at Romero. He attempts to block them before falling on the floor and being stomped on by George's Timberland boots. He manages to grab onto the boot before it hits face, pulling George down to the floor. They pull George up while Romero gets up to run to the bathroom.

They run after him. Romero rushes into the bathroom and enters the last stall. John and his crew follow him, find the stall, and bang on the door.

"You can't stay in there forever!"

Romero looks at the toilet bowl cover and then back at the door as the boys continue to bang on the door and pull on it. He lifts the towel tank cover and puts it on the toilet seat, looking at the gun in the tank.

It's either them or me, but what if the police see you with the gun in your hand? Then what? What if you just scare them until they leave and then put the gun back.

He looks at his watch.

I just got to keep this gun hidden until I see Kalinda.

He grabs the gun out of the toilet bowl and paces while going over the pros and cons of getting caught by the police and scaring off John and his crew.

* * *

Kalinda and Keith arrive at the school wearing all black with hoods over their heads, dark sunglasses, and bandanas covering their faces. She starts walking up the halls, looking in classrooms for Desmond and Thomas. She finds Thomas in class, laughing at a joke being whispered into his ear. The door is slightly cracked open, so she opens it, quietly.

"PSSSSST! Thomas!" she whispers.

He turns around to see who's calling his name. He sees Kalinda in the door, beckoning with her hand. He gets up from his seat and walks out of the class. They dap each other. He sees her brother from a distance, and he acknowledges him with a head nod.

"Where's the strap?"

"We gave it to Romero to hide."

Kalinda looks over to her brother, then back at Thomas.

"Where is he?"

"He should be in Religion with my brother. I'll tell my teacher I'm going to the washroom, and walk you there."

Thomas reenters his class, holding his stomach. He waves to his teacher.

"Yes, Thomas?"

"I'm not feeling so well. I'm gonna go to the bathroom."

"No worries."

"Thanks, Miss."

Thomas exits the room holding his stomach. Once out

of the room, he stands up properly and walks alongside Kalinda. He leads her down the hall.

"This way."

Kalinda and Keith follow him. On their way, they see Desmond walking in the opposite direction. Thomas runs up to Desmond. Kalinda catches up while Keith trails behind.

"Where's pretty boy?" asks Kalinda.

"He went to the washroom and never came back."

"And you never looked for him?"

"What do you think I'm doing now?"

She rolls her eyes, shakes her head in disappointment, and steps back, allowing Desmond to lead her to the washroom.

On entry they see John, Bryson, Victor, and George banging on the door of a stall.

"What are you guys doing?"

Romero stops pacing when he hears Kalinda's voice. He stands on top of the toilet to confirm that it's her. He sees Kalinda, Desmond, and Thomas with a person dressed all in black with their face covered.

"That little pretty boy bitch snuffed me in the hallway earlier. We're here to get payback."

"As long as we're here, he's safe."

"Yeah, and who's going to stop us?"

Keith steps in front of Kalinda. He lowers his bandana to his neck and removes his sunglasses. George takes a step back, stepping on the toes of John. He looks back and mouths "*Sorry.*"

"You know who I am?"

"Look, I got no beef with y'all, but I can't let him get away with snuffing me."

They backpedal as Keith walks toward them. Desmond and Thomas stand back and observe with a smile. The sound of someone whistling from the hallways gets louder.

Keith puts his hand to his ear.

"You hear that? Sound like we're out of time."

Keith cracks his knuckles and takes off his hoodie. They boys look at the veins on his arms and the size of his biceps. George looks at John, Victor, and Bryson, before looking back at Keith.

"You know what? I think it's time we forgive and forget."

The boys quickly run past Keith out of the bathroom.

The door unlocks, and Romero comes out of the washroom with bruises on his face and a fat lip. He hands the gun to Keith.

"I think this belongs to you."

Keith smiles, grabs the gun, and puts it in his pants.

The whistling gets louder. Thomas peeks from the door of the bathroom door and sees Mr. Logan walking down the hall.

"Logan's coming. I'm going to head back to class."

He looks at Desmond and Romero. "I suggest you guys head back to class too, before Logan asks questions."

Thomas and Desmond stop at the door of the bathroom after realizing that Romero isn't behind them. They turn around and watch as Keith and Romero do a handshake.

"Thanks for keeping it safe. If you ever need anything at all," he looks over to Kalinda, "she knows where to find me."

Thomas gestures for Romero to come. Keith and Kalinda hide in bathroom stalls while Romero leaves with Desmond and Thomas. Mr. Logan stops them in the hall. He looks at Romero up and down.

"Man, what happened to you?"

Thomas and Desmond look at Romero, awaiting a response.

"Basketball."

"Sheesh, I hope you make it through the season."

He walks off. The boys look at each other and exhale a huge sigh of relief before heading back to their classes.

* * *

The police leave the school premises after failing to find the weapon.

Romero feels like he has the respect of his friends after coming through for them, but after surviving the assault by the police, he feels he's earned the respect of the rest of his peers.

When Romero arrives home, his younger brother Leonard creeps up at him by the door.

He points the gun at Romero.

BANG!

Romero turns around, startled, causing Leonard to slip and fall. He drops the gun. The safety goes off, and a bullet escapes the gun, breaking a vase in the living room. Romero's eyes widen as he looks at the gun, his brother, and then the vase. He thinks back to the morning when his brother was in his backpack, and everything that happened at school. He puts his finger to mouth.

"*Shhhhh*! I'll tell Mom it was an accident and that I did it, as long as you don't tell her what happened."

Leonard sits on the floor, scared, but nods in agreement. He gets up and runs to his room.

Romero picks up the gun from the floor. He puts the safety on and then puts it in his bag. His mother comes running from the bathroom wrapped in a towel, shower cap still on.

"What was that sound?"

She looks at Romero and then at the broken vase.

"Leonard shot his toy gun. I got startled and accidentally knocked down the vase."

"I can't keep anything for myself. Allya always breaking my shit," she says, shaking her head.

"I'm sorry, Mom, I promise I'll clean it up."

She kisses her teeth, goes back to the bathroom.

"I can't even have a shower in peace," she mumbles.

Romero sighs deeply as he grabs the broom and starts sweeping up the broken vase.

This couldn't be worse.

CHAPTER 16
JUST SOME FRIENDS FROM SCHOOL

Meanwhile, at Kalinda's and Keith's townhouse, Keith is in the kitchen wiping the gun off with a cloth. Kalinda walks in the house and opens the fridge. She grabs a can of pop, opens it, and starts drinking. She exhales a sigh of relief before wiping her mouth.

"I'm so happy this is over with."

Keith attempts to dismantle the gun, but notices something is off when he attempts to clear the chamber. He suddenly realizes the gun is a fake. He grunts out of frustration then whips the gun at Kalinda.

She dodges it, and it hits a glass on the counter. The glass shatters. Kalinda flinches, covering her face. She looks around to see broken glass all over the floor. She walks over the broken glass, grabbing a broom.

"The fuck was that for?"

Keith paces back and forth. "The fucking gun is a fake!"

Kalinda sweeps away the broken glass. "Shit, that means the real gun is still out there."

Keith wags his finger in the air. "We gotta go to your boy's house."

"You think he has the gun?"

"Where else would it be?"

"I'll message Thomas and get the pretty boy's address."

Kalinda reaches into her pocket and grabs her cellphone. She scrolls through her contacts until she finds Thomas's number, then begins to message him: *The gun we retrieved from the school is a fake. We're going to roll up to pretty boy's house and see if he has it.*

Keith laces his Timberland boots and then puts a gun into his pants. Kalinda looks at him, worried.

"Why are you bringing a strap? You don't think he did this on purpose, do you?"

"I don't know what to think. I'm just not leaving this house unprepared. Has your boy responded back with a text yet?"

Kalinda's phone dings. She looks at her phone screen and sees a text from Thomas with an address: *2173 Kipling Ave.*

"Yup, got it."

She walks up to him and shows him the text. They

leave the house, lock the door, and walk to the bus stop.

Romero comes out of his house with a garbage bag. He walks to the back of the house and puts the garbage bag in the bin. He notices his next-door neighbour, a middle-aged white woman, looking at him. He waves. She nods and then walks over to the fence. Romero walks over too.

"What was that loud sound I heard earlier?"

Romero nervously scratches his head. "Sound? What sound?"

"It sounded like a gunshot coming from inside your house."

"Oh, that. That was my brother's toy gun. It can get pretty loud."

"That didn't sound like a toy gun to me."

Romero backs away from the fence. "Well, it was."

"Hmmm, well, I called the cops just to be sure. I wouldn't want anyone getting hurt."

Romero exhales deeply. "You called the cops? Why would you do that? I don't understand why you don't just mind your own business."

"Someone has to keep our community safe, especially with all these minorities moving in."

Romero rolls his eyes, turning his back on her. He walks back into the house. He grabs his school bag and looks inside, verifying that the gun is still there. There's a knock on the door. He exhales deeply.

"What is it now?"

He goes to the door and sees Keith and Kalinda outside on his doorstep.

"WHO IS IT?" his mother yells from the bedroom.

"JUST SOME FRIENDS FROM SCHOOL!"

"TELL THEM THAT YOU CAN'T HANG OUT BECAUSE YOU NEED TO HELP ME COOK DINNER."

Romero opens the door and walks outside with his bag. He closes the door behind him.

"Do you know why we're here?" asks Keith.

Romero lowers his head. He unzips his bag and extends it to Keith. Kalinda pokes her head in the bag and verifies the gun is inside. The neighbour watches intently from over the fence.

"So you holding out on us, pretty boy?"

"Nah, it's not even like that. My stupid kid brother swapped it when I wasn't looking."

Keith puts his hand in the bag and pulls out the gun. The neighbour's eyes widen. She shakes her head. Romero looks at her and rolls his eyes.

"Yo, can you be a bit more discreet? My neighbour watching, and she has the police on speed dial."

Keith looks at her and gives her trigger fingers. Her jaw drops. She goes inside her house and shuts the door. Romero looks at her window and sees her looking through the curtains. Keith cocks the gun to check if it's real.

The police pull into the driveway. Keith and Kalinda

look at each other before looking back at Romero. Keith puts the gun in his pants and runs off. Kalinda follows. The police get out of their cars and chase after them. Romero follows them from a distance.

"STOP!" says an officer.

Keith and Kalinda continue to run. The police officer pulls out his gun and fires a shot. Kalinda falls to the ground. Keith looks back and stops running. He goes back to his sister and holds her up to his chest.

"It's going to be okay."

Tears roll down her face. He wipes them away.

The police approach Kalinda and Keith with their guns pointed.

"Why were you guys running?" asks the police officer.

Keith puts his hands in the air; one officer searches him and finds two guns. He shows his partner and places the guns on the pavement away from Keith and Kalinda. He handcuffs Keith while his partner checks Kalinda for weapons. He inspects the wound.

"She's going to be okay. It went right through her shoulder."

He turns Kalinda over on her stomach and handcuffs her. She winces and groans, bleeding from her shoulder.

Romero stands at a distance, watching the police escort Kalinda and Keith into their cruiser. They are both glowering at him.

Then one of the officers walks over to Romero. Romero

stands in shock, watching as the officer retrieves a pen and notepad.

"Were you the one that called us?"

Romero shakes his head: no.

"Did you know they were armed?"

Romero shakes his head: no.

"How do you know them?"

"School."

Romero's mother comes outside and sees the police cars in her driveway, with Keith and Kalinda sitting inside.

"What's going on?"

"We got a noise complaint. Someone was complaining about a gunshot," says the officer.

Romero's mother frowns at her son; looks to the officer. She then pulls Romero close and whispers in his ear.

"That sound I heard earlier was the gun, and you lied to me. I don't know what happened when I was in the shower, but when these officers leave, I'm going to whoop your ass for lying and embarrassing me in front of all these neighbours. Now go inside. I'll handle the cops."

Romero wipes a tear away as he processes the events, his mother's threat. He walks into the house. From the window he sees his mother talking to the police.

If I stay and wait, she's going to beat me. If I leave, I'll not only avoid the beatings, but I'll be able to start fresh. I wonder what Uncle Stacks is doing. He did say that he wanted to make up for my dad not being here. If I stay with him, he could start making up for my dad not being around.

Romero goes into his room and begins packing clothes into his bag. Leonard comes into the room. He sits on the bottom bunk and watches him pack.

"Why are you packing?"

"Why don't you mind your business for once? You're the reason I'm in this mess."

"Me? What did I do?"

Romero zips up his bag and looks at Leonard. "You went into my bag and took something that didn't belong to you. If you hadn't gone in my bag and taken it, none of this would be happening."

"What's happening?"

Romero kisses his teeth. "You know what? Just leave me alone. I wish you were never born."

Leonard hangs his head and leaves the room. Romero puts on his Allen Iverson jersey, grabs his bag, and makes his way to the living room. He looks out the window; his mother is still talking to the police. He goes through the kitchen and picks up the phone. He dials. It rings a couple times before a man picks up.

"Hello?"

"Uncle Stacks, it's Romero."

"How you doing, Romero?"

"I need your help. Can you meet me at the McDonald's by my school?"

"Sure, is everything all right?"

"Everything is fine, I just need to see you."

"Okay, I'll be there in about twenty minutes."

"Great, I'll see you there."

Romero hangs up and exits the house through the back door. He sees the 45 Kipling bus from a distance.

He looks at his mother still speaking to the officers at the side of the house. The officers walk back to their cars and drive off.

Come on, go inside already.

Romero watches his mother walk into the house before he runs across the street, just making it to the bus stop before the bus takes off.

He gets off at the McDonald's stop and walks into the restaurant. He looks around for his Uncle Stacks and sees him sitting down with a tray full of food. Romero sits down and begins scarfing down fries, then takes a bite of his burger.

"Slow down! I wouldn't want you to choke," says Uncle Stacks, chuckling. "So is everything all right? You said you were in trouble."

Romero wipes his mouth, chews, then swallows.

"The police were at my house today…"

ACKNOWLEDGEMENTS

This book wouldn't have been possible without the support of my wife, thank you for helping me with the kids and giving me the time and space to work. To Allister Thompson thank you so much for believing in me, without you I wouldn't have gotten this opportunity. Thank you for fighting for my voice to be heard and working with me to become a better writer. To my best friend and business partner Jollene Phillips you believed in me when no one else did and for that I am forever grateful. To Justin Key, my friend and mentor, every time I doubted myself you reaffirmed me and inspired me to keep going, this book wouldn't have happened without you, so thank you. To James Lorimer & Company Ltd. Publishers and Palimpsest without your recommendations to the Ontario Art Council, I wouldn't have been able to support myself as an author financially to write this book. Thank you for being the 'Yes' I needed to move forward with accomplishing my dream.